FIRST PRINTING
Maggie's little black
book special edition

WHY BE NORMAL WHEN YOU CAN BE AWESOME?

'Move over Buffy, because monster hunter Maggie Cunningham is in town. THE AWESOME does not merely live up to its name, but in fact, speeds past it at the speed of a crossbow bolt slamming into a vampire's breastbone.'
Chuck Wendig

'Supernatural monster hunting and puberty done right... The story is imaginative, the suspense is taut and the action sequences are worthy of Joss Whedon. I'm onboard for any and all sequels.'
James A. Moore

'I love this book, from cover to cover... What more can I say? I had fun, I loved the characters and the story, and I even got choked up. It was wonderful all around. THE AWESOME delivers exactly what the title promises. Buy it now.'
YA ASYLUM

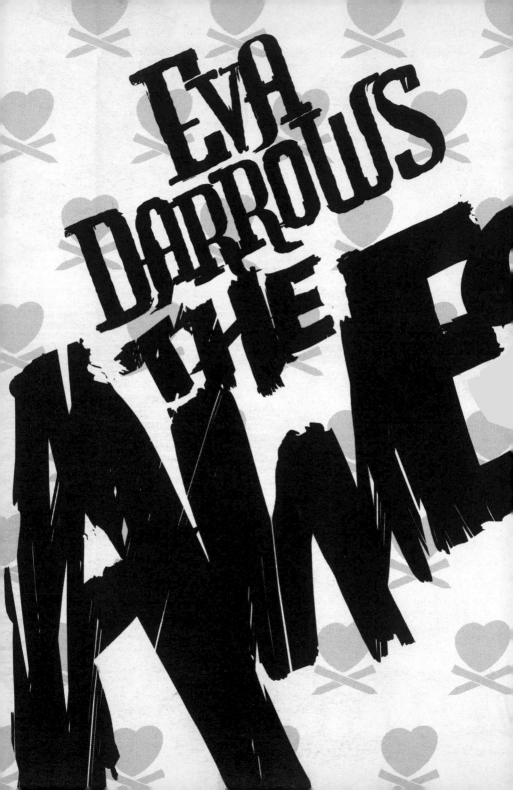

First published 2015 by Ravenstone
an imprint of Rebellion Publishing Ltd,
Riverside House, Osney Mead,
Oxford, OX2 0ES, UK

www.ravenstone.com

US ISBN: 978 1 78108 324 6
UK ISBN: 978 1 78108 323 9

10 9 8 7 6 5 4 3 2 1

A CIP catalogue record for
this book is available from
theBritish Library.

Designed & typeset by
Rebellion Publishing
Cover art by Pye Parr

Printed and bound by
CPI Group (UK) Ltd, Croydon, CR0 4YY

For my mum
who is infinitely cooler than Janice.

CHAPTER ONE

I AM NOT the asskicker people think of when they hear 'monster hunter,' but more on that later.

My name is Margaret Cunningham, though I prefer to go by Maggie because Margaret makes me feel like I'm four hundred years old, and screw that, I'm only seventeen. Cunningham was my father's name, or it was the name he used when he knocked up my mother. The hunting population identity shifts a lot, mostly to keep themselves off the radars of the very monsters they kill. In my dad's case, he died on a werewolf gig before he could give Mom a real, actual name, so Cunningham I was and Cunningham I remain. Around grade school a few of the boys decided it'd be cute to call me Margaret Cunnilingus. Mom says she knew I was destined for hunting greatness when I beat them up at recess, all the while screaming, "Do you want some more?"

Those were the good old days, when life was full of your everyday assholes instead of ghoul, ghost, and golem assholes.

I've been around hunters my whole life, but my apprenticeship didn't start until four years ago, when I was thirteen. Mom decided a poltergeist removal was a great way to break me in, so she took me to a job in scenic Cape Cod, Massachusetts. I remember the house clearly because it was the nicest place I've ever seen. It sat on the bluffs overlooking a picture-perfect private beach. There were three stories of French doors and floor-to-ceiling windows, and every room was packed with antique furniture. Matching his and her Jaguars sat in the driveway—hers was Barbie Corvette pink, and I seriously wanted to key the crap out of it, but Mom would have killed me if I'd touched it.

It was obvious Duffy and Muffy Moneybags were rich, and me and Mom showed up in a bunch of thrift shop dollar bin finds. Hunting is a dirty job; go into it expecting to get covered in something nasty. We headed up the steps, rang the doorbell, and Mrs. Moneybags opened up. She wore Ralph Lauren from head-to-toe, but there was so much ecto dripping from her clothes, it was hard to make out the stitched logo of the dude on the horse. I've seen ectoplasm clear and I've seen it black, and this lady had black all over her, like someone poured a vat of tar over her perfectly-dyed frosty locks.

"You're from the agency?"

"We are. I'm Janice. This is my daughter, Margaret. She's my apprentice and will be helping me with the job today."

"Maggie," I said to no one and everyone.

"Hello, welcome. We seem to have an angry gho..."

She cut off because her husband came screaming around the corner, dripping with so much ecto he looked like a ghost had spooged on him. He hugged a huge blue vase to his chest, sobbed like an infant, and I was pretty sure I saw pee stains on the front of his pants.

"We have an angry ghost," the woman finished.

My mother nodded and stepped inside. "If you'd be kind enough to vacate, we'll take care of that for you."

"Of course. Ronald! We need to go outside!"

Mr. Moneybags, who was apparently also called Ronald, shrieked by in the other direction, this time followed by a phantom blob that glowed a sickly yellow. I'd never seen a ghost in person before, but I was more than ready for it. Mom told me at the tender age of nine that the oogedy boogedy things were all real and Mommy's job was to exterminate them. It was like killing bugs, only in her case, the bugs were nine feet tall and ate human flesh.

I wasn't so much afraid of the spirit as I was fascinated by it. This was what Mom did, it was what my grandparents did, and if I wanted to carry on their completely insane legacy, it's what I'd do, too. Some families had dentistry practices or drywall businesses. Our people hunted monsters and put 'em back in their appropriate crapholes.

"Ronald, honestly. You're embarrassing me."

Ronald's answer was to squawk and barrel-ass past all of us to get to the driveway, still holding the vase like he wanted to make sweet love to it.

"Is the vase, like, his girlfriend or something?"

My mother jabbed me in the boob with her elbow, but not before Mrs. Moneypants cast me a withering look. "It's seventeenth century pottery and the ghost won't leave it alone. He's afraid she'll ruin it."

I would have asked more questions, but the ghost chose that moment to rush us to get to Ronald. It was the first time I'd ever been run through, and let me tell you, you never forget having that particular cherry popped. It's like someone shoving a snow cone down your throat and a popsicle up your butt at the same time. It's hideous, the most invasive thing you can experience this side of the grave. It didn't help that freezing cold ghost goop smeared me from head to toe. My hair was plastered to my scalp, my clothes hung heavy thanks to lumpy black jelly.

"Holy shit! Gross!"

"Maggie!" my mother snapped.

"Holy crap! Gross!"

"Better."

Mom cocked her head to the side like getting ghost-molested *ain't no thang*, watching Ronald run circles around his Jaguar. The ghost stayed in hot pursuit, hands extended and swiping as she hissed. A few times she darted through the car to lunge for him, smearing the glossy exterior and fine leather seats with more goo. I would have cheered if she'd gunked the pink one instead, but that would have scored me another maternal booby-whack, and no thanks, those hurt. "When did the haunting start?"

"Last night," Mrs. Moneypants said, sloughing the freshest layer of ecto from her shoulder. "Around eight."

"When did you get the vase?"

"Yesterday afternoon at auction."

"So it's a haunted item. I need the vase, Mrs. Richmond."

"That vase is worth thirty thousand dollars."

My mother forced a smile so bright, I thought sunshine would blast out her ass like a Care Bear Stare. "It's a thirty thousand dollar haunted item. I can separate the ghost from it, but I need to handle it to do so."

"We don't have it insured yet."

"Oh, well. That changes everything." The sarcasm was palpable, and my mother grabbed my shoulders to face me toward the street. A not-too-gentle shove later and we walked away from the Richmonds and their pretty house. "Good luck with the ghost," Mom called over her shoulder. "If it gets violent, throw salt at it. It'll keep it off of you for a few minutes."

We were nearly to the van before Mrs. Richmond came trotting after us, screeching for us to stop. Mom paused, her expression flat. "Yes?"

"We can't live like this."

"Oh, you can for a while. They don't kill you immediately. Not until they've settled in and decided your house is theirs, anyway."

Mrs. Richmond flinched. "You know what I mean. Please, come back."

"I can handle the vase?"

"Yes, yes, fine. Be careful."

AN HOUR LATER my mother had laid two salt circles five feet apart from one another in the Richmonds' living room. The left one had an incomplete top side; the right was fully sealed and half the size of the first. My mother stood between them, in arm's reach of both, a sack of sea salt in hand. The Richmonds hid behind her, watching the poltergeist rearing at them from the hallway. A line of salt along the threshold kept the ghost at bay. She shrieked her fury, throwing a nutter-fit because she couldn't get to her vase. When I asked Mom why she didn't pass through the walls to get around the salt, she shrugged and said, "They're not real bright."

Good to know.

"I need you to put the vase in the incomplete first circle, Mr. Richmond," Mom said. Ronald didn't look happy about it. As soon as his hands were off the ceramic, he looked like he'd projectile hurl like *The Exorcist* chick on a bender. I retreated a couple feet to avoid heave-range.

"Good. The ghost is fixated on the item, not you, so she will go straight for it when we break the line at the door. You can stand in the second circle for safety if you want. Once she approaches the vase, I'll complete the circle behind her to trap her. At that point, Mrs. Richmond will need to drop the sheet to block out the light."

The windows in the room were covered by flattened moving boxes, the edges sealed off with Duck Tape. The aforementioned sheet was tacked above the door, ready to be dropped as soon as a strategically-placed strip of tape was removed. I was on salt-breaking duty and UV duty. I foisted the light to let my mother know I was ready. I'd read all about ghost banishments, and my mother had talked my ear off about them, but the actual doing was way more exciting than secondhand stories. I was so stoked my nipples were hard, like I'd smuggled raisins in my bra.

"... what if she hurts the vase?"

"Shut up, Ronald," Mrs. Richmond snarled. "I'm not living with that thing any longer than necessary."

"Stuff it, Missy."

I coughed into my shoulder, fairly certain if I let out a full-throttle cackle my mother would whale me upside the head with the salt bag.

"All right, let's do this. Margaret, the salt line please." I glowered at her to let her know what I thought of her using my full name, and she winked at me, nodding towards the poltergeist. I approached the doorway, extending my leg as far as it would go. The moment my sneaker broke the line, the poltergeist raced past me. I barely got out of her way before she swirled around the vase, trilling and cooing like Gollum with his precious. My mother shook salt onto the floor behind her, but the ghost ignored her, too intent on the vase to notice. Mom double checked her circle then motioned at Mrs. Richmond.

"Let it down, please. Maggie, into the corner. Don't turn on the light until I say."

I put my back to the wall, waiting for the darkness. There was a *fwoosh* as the sheet dropped, and the room went black save for the yellowish glow of the ghost. Her spectral hands coursed over the vase, sometimes passing through it, sometimes going solid enough to rock it on its base. Whenever it teetered, Ronald whimpered, sounding a lot like he'd weep again.

What a nerd.

"All right. Go."

I flicked the switch on the light and waited. The idea behind this particular ghost trap was simple: we recreated the light people saw when they died, giving the illusion of Heaven. Most ghosts were people who missed the afterlife boat the first time around because they were too busy picking their noses or sniffing their armpits to notice. Or, you know, had died so violently they were too freaked out to do anything other than flail. The UV light was bright enough and brilliant enough that it looked celestial in a dark room and, if the ghost *believed* it was the mighty hereafter, that was enough to shepherd them on. Mom said she'd gotten the ultimate pain of a ghost one time who refused to cross over because he liked being a turdburger to the people in 'his' house, but that was a rarity. Most spirits wanted peace; they just needed a few theater props to get there.

The poltergeist stopped caressing the vase to ogle the light, drawn like a bug to a zapper. Since she wasn't writhing, spitting, or hosing anyone down with ecto, I got my first good look at her. She wore old-timey clothes, like maybe she came from the same era as the vase. If that was the case, maybe it had been her most prized possession when she was alive, or maybe it was in the room with her when she died.

I wasn't given long to ponder it. The poltergeist drifted to the edge of her salt circle and smiled, her hand extending toward the light. She flared bright and expanded, brilliant like a star, and then she poofed from existence, her only remnant a cloud of acrid-smelling smoke.

NOT TO BRAG or anything, but it was a pretty fantastic way to start my illustrious spook-hunting career. The Richmonds had their vase back, I'd officially become an apprentice hunter, and Mom was five thousand dollars richer. Sadly, flawless victory didn't stop Mom from getting on me like a fat kid on cake as soon as my butt hit the passenger's side seat of the van.

"What's the first thing I said to you before we left the house this morning?" She demanded, pulling out a pack of Nicorette and stuffing her cheeks until they bulged. I was pretty sure she wasn't supposed to have four pieces at once, but Mom had been doing whatever the hell she pleased for as long as I could remember, so why would this be any different?

"That the van smelled like a dead dog's bunghole."

"Okay, point. What was the second thing I said to you?"

I rolled my eyes. "Don't swear in front of the clients. Look, I'm sorry, but that was the grossest thing, like, ever. It came out before I could stop it."

She popped Hendrix into the CD player, cranking it loud. The van's wheels shredded rubber over the Richmond's driveway. "I get it," she said, shouting to be heard over the music. "It's skeevy to be run through. But keep a lid on it next time. The only reason I'm not chewing out your ass is because they were a pair of douchecanoes, and I could give a damn what they think of us."

"What's a douchecanoe, Mommy?"

"Don't know, but it has a ring to it, don't you think?"

I had to admit, it sorta did.

CHAPTER TWO

So, AS I said earlier, I am not the asskicker folks picture when they hear 'monster hunter.' For starters, I don't own leather pants. "What respectable bad-ass doesn't own leather pants?" you may ask. This one right here. I don't own a single pair, and if I did? You wouldn't want to see me in them. There'd be lumps all over the place and a muffin top that resembles peach cottage cheese.

I also don't wear tall boots. They're impractical. Have you ever tried running in anything with heels, or for that matter, anything squeezing your calves like sausage casings? When you fight monsters, you tend to do a lot of short distance sprinting, and if my life depends on my capacity to get out of Dodge, I want sneakers with a good tread and nothing else. You know those horror movies where the silicon-inflated babe totters down the street in stilettos while a werewolf lopes after her at six thousand miles an hour? All I have to say to that is, "Bitch would have gotten away if she'd picked better shoes."

So, no leather pants, no tall boots. Oh, no wife-beaters or tank tops either because exposing the arms is *stupid*. Monster Z with Huge Claws should have to go through something quasi-dense before it gets to maul my flesh. Call me a wussy, it's okay! But I am all in favor of being intact at the end of a monster fight, not looking like I was spit out of a paper shredder. Getting raked, clawed, bitten, swiped, and maimed hurts. Inviting further injury by compromising practicality for style is... well it's stupid, like I said.

What do I wear? Comfortable, broken-in jeans that let me move, a pair of antique sneakers, and a lot of ratty, hoodless sweatshirts. My hair is cut short because long locks give a monster something to grab onto, and I like being handle-free. It's also brown, like baby crap brown, which is boring but I'm fine with that.

To answer a few of the standard questions about hunters and hunting in general: Can I throw a dagger from three miles away and hit a bullseye? No. Do I own a sniper rifle? No, but Mom does. Can I disconnect a bomb, or for that matter, build a bomb out of Bisquick? No. Sword fighting, no. Scaling walls like Spider-Man, roof jumping, hacking into mainframe computers, making Jason Bourne look like a loser: No, no, no, and maybe on the last, but that's only in ideal conditions and if he were a vampire.

Well, maybe if he were a vampire.

Okay, probably not if he were a vampire. There was this whole thing about me going on vampire hunts.

"Not 'til you get laid."

I watched my mother make her twenty-seventh cup of coffee that day and frowned. "Oh, come on! All I need is a fang kill for journeyman and you're holding me back. Actually, you're holding *us* back. We'd get better rates if I get certified."

"Don't put this on me, kid. You're seventeen. Most kids your age are getting their sex on. Not my fault you're holding onto the almighty hymen." I picked up a spoon and chucked it at her, and she batted it away with a tut, flashing me one of her awful Cheshire Cat grins. "Temper, temper."

"Where am I supposed to meet kids my age? I'm home-schooled, remember?"

"And whose fault is that, Miss 'I'm going to beat Joey What's-His-Nuts's face against the monkey bars 'til I knock out his front teeth'? Next time you decide to teach someone a lesson, don't make it the superintendent's grandson." She flopped into the computer chair with her coffee, dumping a bunch of powdered creamer into it. "And I'm getting sick of this conversation, Maggie. You know the rules. No sex, no vampire hunt. They're tough enough to kill without a frenzy."

The problem with vampires is they love virgins, and not in the biblical humpy-humpy way. They love to eat them. Apparently, they can smell someone's innocence—unplucked flesh contains the sweetest blood—and when they catch a whiff, they go nuts to get their hands on it. The older ones learn to suppress the urge, but the fledglings... well. It's ugly. As vamps are stronger and faster than humans, roid-raging them up for virgin blood doesn't exactly tip the odds in the hunter's favor, which meant until I did the nasty with a dong of my choosing, I was a liability. Sadly, it had to be flesh in flesh sex to count as a true deflowering, so cheating with a battery operated boyfriend wouldn't make the trip.

"I could sit in the car while you kill it," I said hopefully.

"Right, because they don't have super senses or anything. The answer is no, Margaret. If you want it so bad, go get 'er done. And if you don't use a condom, I'll kill you."

"You're gross. You're setting women's lib back by, like, fifty billion years."

She fired up the computer, plunking in her password and waiting for the home screen to load. "Yep, that's me. Anti-feminism. A weak wallflower who wants you to debase yourself before a man. Oh, while we're on the subject, why don't you take your shoes off and go make me a meatloaf? I'm starving."

"Screw you."

"Love you too, baby girl!"

"Hey. Hey wait a minute." I narrowed my eyes, looming over her desk like I'd become one of those creepy guys who rub against girls on packed trains. "Allie Silva's a lesbian."

"And?"

"So how's she a hunter?"

When my mother's smile gets to a certain point, I know whatever she's about to do or say is going to result in cry time, and right then, she smiled so wide the corners of her mouth nearly touched her ears. She lifted up her left hand and made a circle. With the other hand, she crammed fingers through the circle until it couldn't hold them anymore. I didn't get it at first, and then I did, and I felt my eyes bulge from my skull, like one of those rubbery dolls that explode from their eyes, mouth, and bum when you squeeze their middle. "NO WAY! You're such a freak. You are *such* a freak."

"Hey, you asked. And if you're not up for the boys, you're more than welcome to find yourself a nice girl. I'm hip, I'm happening, I am totally down with you crazy kids exploring your sexuality. I love you no matter what, Margaret Jane Cunningham. Gimme a kiss." She kissy faced at me and I swatted her away, sitting down in the overstuffed chair next to the desk. She continued to quasi-molest me until the computer came alive and Monster Finder popped up on the monitor.

Monster Finder (or MFer if you're juvenile like me and liked swear words a lot) was how we did our job. It was a reporting database linked to the DoPR, or Department of Paranormal Relations. A hunter put in their territory number, and MFer would spit out a report on the monsters in our area that needed attending. Some days there'd only be a name or two there, others days there'd be a dozen. Each case was ranked according to difficulty: one star jobs were the easy ones—low grade ghosts, house brownies (which my mother called car key gnomes)—while five stars were the kill on sight dangerous jobs. You found a lot of rogue vampires and werewolves in the four and five star range, monsters that not only refused to register with the DoPR but also exhibited violent behavior. Sometimes hunters from different territories would team up and split the profits from the five star jobbies. They paid the best for obvious reasons, and in my mother's case, she usually called Allie Silva and her partner, Tiny Tina for three-way hunting fun.

The 'Tiny' part of Tina's name was ironic: the woman could lose fifty pounds and it'd be like throwing the deck chairs off of the *Titanic*. She was three tons of hunting love.

"What do we have here?" Mom printed up the list and skimmed it, eyes flickering over the assignments. There were only three jobs today, unusual for a Saturday, and I knew without asking the top job would go untouched, so it was more like two jobs. Jeffrey Sampson, a one star vampire whose only crime was refusing to register with the DoPR and thus needed to be tagged with a tracer, had been popping up for the better part of a year, but every time I mentioned him, Mom shooed me off. She said tagging jobs paid poorly, and the best way to get a one star vampire job escalated to a five star job was to plant a bug on someone who didn't want it. The risk wasn't worth the pay.

"Looks like a werewolf ate Red Riding Hood's grandma out in Hingham and a four star vamp attack in Peabody. Gotta call Allie."

"So what am I supposed to do all night?" Being an apprentice, even a fourth year apprentice, I couldn't touch anything over a three star job or my mother would lose her hunting license. This translated to Mom taking off for an overnight werewolf gig while I stayed at home to watch brain-numbing reality television.

"Oh, I dunno. Study for your GED? Or maybe you can go somewhere where there are people your own age and pretend you're normal." She grinned as she reached for the phone. "Of course, TLC does have that show about people who eat their hair..."

"Normal. Right. Hey pot, this is kettle. You're black."

"I'm normal enough!"

"The kids in school used to call you the diesel dyke." It was supposed to be a dig, but by her awful smirk, I could tell I'd missed my mark.

Back when I slogged through the dredges of angst otherwise known as junior high, my classmates thought I was a freak factory partially because I was one, but mostly because my mother was so *out there*. Every time they saw her she had different colored hair: pink, purple, sometimes green and blue. She wore military-issued combat boots, and drove either a white kidnapper van, a huge F-150 pickup truck, or a motorcycle. She was part rock star, part ninja, the secret love child of Lady Gaga and Jet Li. My friends didn't know if they should be scared of her or worship at the shrine of Janice, so they did both to cover their bases.

"You're so jealous of me," she said. "Seriously though. You talk to Julie, right? Call her and see if she's going out tonight. It'll do you good to do something fun for once."

"But hunting's fun." I picked up her coffee to bogart a sip, scrunching my face in a pucker when I realized she hadn't sweetened it.

"Okay, something fun and not dangerous."

"But dangerous is fun."

"Margaret. Stop being a pain in the ass."

"Fiiiine."

Mom wandered into the other room with her phone. I listened to her hash out the details of that night's job with Allie, all the while stealing misery-inducing gulps of her coffee. I was far too lazy to get the sugar from the kitchen. It was a whole ten feet away, and my chair was too comfortable to vacate. Instead I suffered through bitter crap-in-a-cup, working myself into a snit when Mom talked about cool stuff like crossbows and silver bullets.

"This sucks."

Not wanting to sit at home brooding about the life-threatening fun fest I couldn't attend, I picked up my burner phone, one of those jobbies you bought at 7-11 with prepaid minutes, and called my old friend Julie. Who was I kidding? She was my only friend. But one friend was better than no friends or so I told myself. I wasn't telling Mom this, nor would I tell Julie, but if I could sucker an invite into Julie's plans, I was on a mission. I, Margaret Cunningham would try my hand at being a slutbag.

Because ready or not, Maggie needed a promotion.

CHAPTER THREE

THERE I WAS at eight o'clock, tarted up like a Ru Paul wanna-be, waiting for Julie. I'd used Snooki's "two bras for extra cleavage" tip that I saw on TV, and my boobs bobbed somewhere between my chin and my eyebrows. I'd attacked my face with eyeliner, mascara, and lipstick, and somehow managed to come out not looking like a clown. This was a vast improvement over my last venture in being a girl, wherein my mother had used words like "hooker on hallucinogens" to describe my appearance. I loved her, but when she was mean, she made Attila the Hun look soft.

Allie and Tina arrived around suppertime, both of them poster children for the NRA with their big, impressive guns and camo. I couldn't help but notice Allie's new eye patch; considering it covered half her face, I'd have to be blind *not* to notice. She offered an explanation without prompting, her nicotine-stained teeth clenching on the end of her cigarette in what could be construed as a grin. By the slightly feral curl of her upper lip, I wouldn't risk putting a hand near her mouth. I valued my fingers.

"A sidhe ripped it out last week," she said. "Took his time digging around the socket with his finger, too. Made me watch him eat it afterward. Always hated those sons of bitches."

That was all she said of it, heading out to the van and waiting for her partners. I stared after her, trying to imagine a lithe, glorious fae with its pretty hair and pointy ears eating someone's freshly plucked eyeball. Tiny Tina snickered, clapping a ham hand on my shoulder as she passed me by.

"She's got pink eye. Don't be so gullible."

"Oh, right. I totally knew that," I said, though both Tina and I knew I'd bitten hook, line, and sinker. Allie liked to haze me. The problem was she wove lies into her regular conversation so seamlessly, I had no idea what was up and what was down. One time she told me about getting punched in the kidney by a rabid leprechaun, I'd called her on it, and was promptly presented with actual cell phone footage of a frothing-mouthed green man moaning and kicking while he got stuffed into a sack.

Who knew?

"Have fun tonight," Mom said, tugging a baseball cap over her pink hair and reaching for her crossbow. "There's leftover pizza in the fridge if you get hungry. Don't be an asshat to Julie. Say 'please' and 'thank you' and all that other happy horseshit. Okay?"

"Uh huh."

"Love you."

She blew me a kiss and trotted for the van. Watching the taillights disappear over the crest of the street made me melancholy. I should have been with them, beating up werewolves and vampires, hurling holy water grenades and firing guns. I was a hunter, damn it, not some useless sack of lame wallowing in self-pity on a Saturday night.

There was only one way to ensure I wouldn't be left behind again: *the virginity had to go.* If I couldn't be a hunter tonight, I'd be a master seductress—a wily, conniving minx who'd lure some unsuspecting boy into my baited trap. I'd charm him with a smile and my witty banter. I'd be the type of girl every guy dreamed of with my ridiculously buoyant boobs and too-tight jeans. What did it matter if I didn't associate with kids my age? I'd seen all of Megan Fox's crappy high school movies. I watched *Glee* reruns. Everything I needed to know about being seventeen I'd learned from TV.

How hard could it be?

SHORT ANSWER: HARD. Longer answer: Julie picked me up a full half hour later than she told me she would. I would have pretended to be surprised, but I wasn't that good of a bullshit artist. I'd been hanging out with the girl since grade school and she'd never been on time for a single thing. When I was nine years old, Janice got the bright idea to take me and a few of my school friends to Chuck E. Cheese's for my birthday. I woke up at something like six in the morning, so excited I'd get to see the Chuck-E-Cheese logo rat I ran around the house in circles and screamed my head off. Mom'd chewed through a pack and a half of Nicorette by noon that day, finally snapping and saying if I didn't cut the crap, she'd feed me to the bridge troll on Nantucket. As bridge trolls crapped bigger than me, I believed her, settling in front of the TV to watch cartoons until it was time to go.

Everything was cool until Julie's Mom called us to tell us that, "Julie'd lost track of time, they'd be about an hour late." I'd gone ballistic, of course, because an hour was forever to a kid, and I'd built Chuck E. Cheese's up to be the mecca of childhood fun. Mom's solution was to let me open my birthday presents right away, thus placating me long enough for Julie to get there.

It baffles me how a nine-year-old kid with the promise of pizza, slushies, video games, and a big dancing rat 'loses track of time,' but somehow, Julie managed it. Nearly ten years later, she still managed it. She lost at least fifteen or twenty minutes of time every day as far as I could tell.

"Nice of you to show up, wench," I said, climbing into the side of her car. A quick glance her way and I immediately felt under-dressed. Her hair looked salon styled, her makeup was perfect. She had on a sassy skirt with crinkly fabric and a halter top, like she'd pointed at a fashion magazine and went "Yes, that" and POOF! it was on her body. It served to prove how different we were; I padded around the house in ancient sweatpants and tee shirts; she wouldn't be caught dead in anything non-designer. She got paraffin wax manicures; I dug crusted blood and ectoplasm out from under my nails with a dagger.

Somehow we maintained a friendship, though. Part of it I chalked up to opposites attracting, part of it was she'd always been obsessed with me and Janice's lifestyle. She thought we were the coolest of the cool with all our guns and glory. Also, she liked vampires. She totally bought into the Edward Cullen sparkly vampire crap and she knew Mom got to interact with real ones. I liked her too much to tell her how brutal and disgusting fangers were; let her have her pretty Robert Pattinson illusions.

"Uhh, should I change?" I asked. "I figured house party so jeans, but if I need something fancier... "

"You're fine. I'm meeting John there and I wanted to wear something cute." She grinned and leaned over the steering wheel to peer at the house. "Is Janice home? I'll go say 'hi.'"

"Nope. Off on a werewolf hunt with the rest of the Bitches of Eastwick. Won't be home 'til tomorrow."

"Bummer. Guess we're set to go then."

She pulled out of the driveway and headed towards the main road. I figured I should ask about this John person she mentioned, though trying to keep track of her boyfriends required a super powered computer and a doctorate from MIT. There were too many names and faces to process. She juggled boys like a circus performer juggled flaming balls—skillfully and without fear. "Who's John? I thought you were seeing Mike."

Julie's face puckered as soon as I said the name. "Mike was boring and emo. Not my bag, but it's cool 'cause I met John through Ian a couple weeks ago. Ian's my cousin, the one having the party. My aunt and uncle are off in Sedona doing some weird astral flight thing so we're holding down the fort while they're gone."

'Holding down the fort' was apparently synonymous with 'have a huge house party and get your friends drunk' which I was totally cool with. I had a plan, see—a flawless plan to have The Sex. Parties and The Sex went hand in hand almost as closely as watching *Xena* reruns and questioning my sexuality.

"Astral flight? Like... bow-wicca-wicca astral flight?"

"Yeah, you know. You stuff."

I peered at her from the corner of my eye. "Just because it's got magic associated with it doesn't mean it's 'me stuff.'"

"Well, yeah, but you're into strange stuff, so I figured you'd at least know what astral flight is. It sounds super freaky to me. Like, I don't... whatever. My aunt and uncle are weird. I feel bad for Ian."

I wanted to correct the "you're into strange stuff" thing to "you're into awesome stuff" but I was too pure of a soul to do that to my nearest, dearest, and only friend. "I guess.

Your idea of freaky and mine are way different. Like, rabid leprechauns? Freaky. Totally freaky, dude."

"Wait, what?"

We spent the next twenty minutes blabbing about random stuff. I explained the leprechaun thing, she told me about her high school—mostly about her being a runner up for Prom Queen and how "Lily Petronelli is such a bitch and totally didn't deserve to win." I nodded and pretended I cared, which seemed to be enough for her because she talked about it non-stop for another ten minutes. I was given a reprieve when she turned the car into a nice, upper class neighborhood, announcing we were only a couple minutes away from Ian's house. My bladder thanked her for that; I'd had about thirty thousand cups of coffee over the course of the day and I needed to break the seal.

"Man, I have to wizz like a racehorse," I announced. "Like, whoa bad pee time. Wish I'd thought of this earlier."

Julie eased the car onto the curb of the street, a smirk oozing across her mouth. "You're so weird, Maggie." She flipped on the interior light of her Ford Focus to check her makeup, turning her face this way and that to ensure she looked Top Model gorgeous. "You say the strangest stuff. It's cool—you're funny—but you're strange." She skimmed the tip of her finger around her mouth to capture any unappealing smudges, and then did Duck Face. Duck Face was supposed to be a 'come hither' kissy pucker thing, but it more resembled a genetic deformity. I was pretty sure if I wanted The Sex, Duck Face was not the way to go.

"Yeah, well, I'm not the girl whose aunt is off licking a cactus for spiritual growth."

"That's on my aunt, not me. Ian's normal, thank God. I think you'll like him. He's one of those brooding quiet types."

* * *

I WASN'T SURE what part of my disposition suggested I liked brooding quiet types, but the six condoms in my pocketbook told me to shut the hell up and go with it. If Julie said I'd like him, like him I would if for no other reason than he was male and had a wang.

"By the way, love the haircut," she said, getting out of the car. "It's pixie cute."

"Oh, thanks."

"That Hermione girl wore it like that too. What's her... Emma something. You know, from *Potter*? I couldn't do it, but you've got the face for it."

I had no idea what she meant, but I nodded emphatically regardless, following her through the front door and into a den of decadence. There had to be forty kids here, some milling around the living room talking, others standing sentry by the keg in the kitchen. Music blared, hip-hop stuff I couldn't name because my mother wouldn't listen to anything recorded past 1990, and the lights were kept dim if not on purpose, then by shirts and coats strewn haphazardly over table lamps. Red and blue plastic cups seemed to be the token party favor. I could tell by the smell no one was getting down with their bad, ginger-aled selves tonight. It reeked like a brewery already, and it wasn't nine yet.

"Bathroom's over there," she pointed, and I pushed through a sea of bodies to take care of the pee problem. A thorough examination of my reflection in the medicine cabinet later, I walked back out, looking for Julie's shiny blond head. She was in the kitchen, hugging some tall skinny guy with spiky black hair. I hoped she'd be decent enough to introduce me. I knew no one, and though I wasn't exactly a shrinking violet, I wasn't so ballsy as to say a foot-in wouldn't be appreciated.

"Oh hey. Maggie, over here. This is my cousin Ian."

I craned my head back and smiled. Ian was tall, like 6'4" tall, and though I was 5'7", he made me feel dumpy, like I stood in a hole.

"'Sup," Ian said. I expected something more beyond a three letter greeting, but apparently that was all I would get. He was too busy guzzling beer and looking down my shirt to muster anything else.

Stare away, dude, and while we're at it, let me introduce the girls. Perky left and slightly perkier right, which makes me self-conscious when I'm naked. Not that I'd tell you that or anything.

"'Sup," I said back.

It was weird the times my mother's advice reared its ugly head. There I was, standing in the kitchen surrounded by my fellow teenage man, and Mom's voice piped into my brain, like she'd pressed play on a recording. "The best way to bag a monster is to fit into your surroundings. Look like you belong there, imitate what you see. If you're in a public venue, don't be conspicuous. Keep your head down and your ears cracked. For that matter, listen more than talk, and never, ever let your guard down."

Okay, so if it worked for hunting monsters, it could work for hunting guys. Right?

"Cool party," I blurted out before I could remind myself about the whole 'listening more than talking' thing.

"Thanks. You want a beer?"

"Sure."

"Jules?"

"'Course."

A plastic cup found its way into my hand, and I stared at the foamy contents with something akin to dread. When I was fifteen, I made the mistake of asking Mom if I could have a sip of her Heineken. She responded by putting the twelve pack on the kitchen table and telling me to go to town, that beer drinking was a rite of passage, and she was happy to be my copilot. Thinking I was Queen Crap of Turd Mountain, I drank one, and then two, and before I knew better, eight. I didn't like the taste but because drinking made me feel older and awesomer by its very nature, I sucked 'em down like a stoner on a taco-binge.

I remember nothing about being drunk—I must have blacked out around the fifth beer—but when I woke up the next day, I proceeded to paint the walls of my bedroom with vomit. The puking was bad enough, but Mom's subsequent insistence that I clean up my mess *right then* combined with Ozzy's "Crazy Train" played so loudly it shook the walls meant that I swore off alcohol forever.

This beer, though the first ever served to me at my first ever party, didn't interest me in the slightest.

In an attempt to blend in, I took a tiny sip, stopping myself from making a blech face. Blech face rivaled Duck Face in ugly, and I aimed for sex siren, not a *Cosmo* top ten list of Things Not To Do To Impress A Guy.

I was about to attempt lamer small talk with Ian again, hoping to engage him in a battle of wits that would dazzle Plato himself, but a kid with a shaved head came into the kitchen and helped himself to a beer, essentially cock-blocking me.

Or would that be vag-blocking me?

"Hey. Melissa coming?"

Ian finished off his beer and poured another. "We broke up last week."

"Shit, man. Sorry to hear it."

"It's cool."

It made me a bad person, but I could have done cartwheels right about then. Ian was not only single, he was rebounding, which boded well for random, bumbling hookups with career-minded young women such as myself. Hopefully he didn't think I was gross. I wasn't ugly or anything, but I knew I was rounder than I should be, and in comparison to the normal standards of beauty—a la Julie who had everything going for her ever, the douchebag—I seemed plain with my brown eyes and brown hair. Ian was a good-looking guy, and though I'd known him for all of five minutes, I'd pinned my hopes on him being The One, but that hinged on him deciding I wasn't a swamp beast from Hell.

The good news for me? He alternated between drinks and blatant peeks down my shirt. Shaved head guy kept talking to him, and Ian would shrug or nod answers here and there, but he focused on me pretty hardcore. Julie noticed it, too. She caught my eye, grinned, and gave me a wink that would have done my mother proud.

That should have been my first sign that I was screwed, and not in the way I'd planned.

CHAPTER FOUR

BY ELEVEN O'CLOCK, Ian walked me around the house with his arm slung over my shoulders. I discovered something important that night: the ratio of alcohol consumed would, over time, equate to willingness to engage other human beings in conversation. His answers went from one and two words to four and five words, eventually evolving into full sentences and dialogue. The strange part was none of it was directed *at me*, but he lugged me around with him anyway, every once in a while pulling me into his conversations with a well-timed "Right?" or a "Hey, meet Maggie. She's pretty cool." He had no idea if I was cool or not because he hadn't actually talked to me, but whatever, I wasn't picky. This wasn't Romeo and Juliet. It was 'drunken shenanigans and you won't respect me in the morning.' I hadn't set my expectations very high.

Over the next hour, he drank some more, and then more after that, socking beer away like it was the nectar of life. When he high-fived random dudes—basketball teammates, Julie said when she swept by to check on me—I knew we'd gone from 'a little buzzed' to full on drunk. This assertion proved itself when he ran over to some guy whose name started with L and dry humped him from behind while making woo woo noises.

Yeah, I knew how to pick 'em.

Apparently making L-guy his bitch put him in a mood. When he came back my way, he bent down to whisper into my ear that I was pretty. It seemed so random; one minute he butt slapped some dude, the next he told me I was pretty. A glib part of me wanted to point out exactly what a leap that was, but that wouldn't win me any points, and as Imaginary Head Janice said, "Listen more, talk less." So I shut my mouth and smiled, which he must have taken as encouragement because he took my hand and pulled me towards the stairs. He weaved around his guests, nodding at some, "'sup"ing others, and pausing only once to take a shot of whiskey with the team captain.

The next thing you know, we climbed towards the great unknown. It was weird; the whole night I'd hoped for this, planned on it, really, but now that I went somewhere alone with him, I felt nauseated. It wasn't a shame thing so much as a worry that he'd find me lacking, and oh God, what would he think if he took off my shirt and saw two black bras instead of one? I should have realized taking fashion tips from Snooki would result in disaster.

She's Snooki, for Christ's sake.

I cast a frantic glance behind me to look for Julie and saw her sitting in some guy's lap in the corner, talking to six people at once. They laughed and smiled and drank, acting like kids ought to act, and for a moment I wished I was over there next to her, hanging out and being normal. The fact was, though, I wasn't normal. I was a hunter, I was the daughter of a hunter, and that meant I was atypical in every way, shape, and form.

Oh God, form. Get the second bra off, stupid.

Ian led me to a room, his room if I had to guess by the Celtics poster on the door. I stopped short, looking down the hall at a second bathroom. A celestial choir ought to have descended from the heavens to sing Hallelujah then, because I'd been handed an opportunity to de-bra myself before I looked like a total jerkoff in front of this new guy.

"Hey, give me two seconds? Need to hit the bathroom."

He nodded and smiled, cracking the door and backing inside. "I'll be here."

"You better be."

It was supposed to be flirty and funny, but it came out threatening, like I'd punch him in the sack if he changed his mind. Good thing the booze dulled his senses too much to notice, though for all I knew he was stupid and hadn't picked up on it. I hoped that wasn't the case. I'd like to have something good to say about the guy that de-virginized me other than, "well, his hair spikes were equidistantly spaced and he had a decent smile."

I wriggled out of the second bra and checked my makeup, sweeping the back of my hand across my forehead to rid myself of the sweat. I was more nervous than I wanted to admit, but I wasn't backing out now. Hell, at that point I didn't know if this was going anywhere. He could want to talk or make out or show me his stamp collection. No sense in assuming this was it, though I secretly prayed it was. I wanted to get it over with. Don't get me wrong, I liked hanging out with Julie, and it had been an interesting night if not exactly fun, but I didn't want to have to keep doing this to score myself a promotion. That felt like I used Julie for her network of normal people, which was shady. Plus? She looked kinda happy talking to everyone downstairs. It'd be nice to think the next time we did this, if there was a next time, I could sit on the couch and participate in the hang out instead of gluing myself to some random guy's side.

"Totally fine. I got this," I mumbled, doing a cursory pit sniff to make sure I didn't stink. I spotted a can of Lysol, and I toyed with the idea of giving myself spritzes underneath my arms, but Ian probably wasn't so drunk he wouldn't notice that I smelled like antibacterial bathroom spray.

I stood up straight and breathed hard, steeling myself for whatever awaited me in the other room.

I could do this. I was *strong*. I was *awesome*.

I was scared to death.

IT OCCURRED TO me halfway between the bathroom and Ian's room that I had problems beyond the nerves thing, namely logistics. For one I'd never kissed anyone before. The movies made it look pretty easy; there were a lot of lingering gazes and glimpses of tongue, and I supposed the rule of mimicry applied here. If he did it first, it was okay for me to do it back, and if he didn't like it, he had no one to blame but his own dumb ass.

The second concern was endowment. Under the premise that I was quasi-small in the bits thanks to my inexperience, was I in for ultimate pain? Not only was Ian tall, but he had huge feet, and there was some stupid thing about junk size correlating to foot size. I'd liked to have dismissed it as an old wives' tale, but the last time I'd dismissed something that sounded ridiculous, I got rabid leprechaun video thrust in my face.

I put my hand on Ian's door and pushed it open, getting my first good look at his room. Besides basketball posters, he had a bunch of velvet paintings, the kind with neon paints so they'd glow under a black light. Some were skulls with snakes, others were funky, psychedelic patterns. I wasn't sure why, but I was disappointed he hadn't turned on a black light. I wanted to see everything purple and bright. I looked around, and sure enough I spotted the long cylinder bulb above a wall mirror covered in baseball cards. I walked over and snapped it on, hoping he wouldn't yell at me for touching his stuff without invitation.

He didn't. Instead he killed the lamp at his bedside and sat down on his mattress, smiling at me. Though his teeth glowed eerie white, it was better like this, less scary in the dark. Maybe he wouldn't see that I was about to crap pickles all over his floor.

"Everything's awesomer with black light."

He slurred the sentence so badly I flinched. That didn't stop me from approaching him, standing a foot and a half away from his bed. He extended a long arm to wrap his fingers around mine, pulling me between his splayed knees.

"You're cool, Meggie."

"... Maggie."

"S'what I said."

I wouldn't argue with a drunk dude mainly because, well, he was drunk, but also because he pulled me in close. The nausea from the stairs returned tenfold. It wasn't that he wasn't cute, or that he smelled like he'd bathed in a vat of beer, though that wasn't the most attractive thing in the world. It was that this thing that was happening, whatever it was, might be standard fare for him, but it was foreign to me. I had no idea what I was doing. Sure, I was good at a lot of stuff. How many girls my age could kill a dude with her bare hands in under fourteen seconds? That's a skill, and one that'd get me places in life, but it didn't help me here. All the combat training in the world couldn't make being a normal teenager any easier.

Megan Fox was full of crap.

A hand crept around the back of my neck to pull me down. Ian's hot breath brushed over my lips for a moment, and then I got kissed. My first kiss. I'd read horror stories about this in magazines; some guys had breath like a dragon, some guys used so much tongue it was like making out with a golden retriever. Though Ian tasted beery, he was sweet and gentle, not forceful or drooly in the slightest. In fact, there was no tongue at all at first, just this pleasant mouth massage type thing that got me pretty well acquainted with the bow in his upper lip. Eventually tongue got involved, yes, but it wasn't a saliva fest. It was all... nice and stuff.

I slid my hands over his shoulders and concentrated on kissing him back, letting my eyes flutter closed. I figured if he glanced up to see me staring at him like he'd grown a second head it'd be a mood killer, so I went with it. My copycat approach to making out must have done the trick— he made this weird grunty noise in the back of his throat, his fingers sliding from my neck to my back, and then to my butt. Lo and behold, I grunted back. Sad but true, pursuit of The Sex made me fall off the evolutionary train twelve stops too early.

After a while he pulled away, swaying back and forth even though he sat. His breathing came hard, and I realized (much to my chagrin) mine did too. I'd liked it. In the vast scheme of my devirgining plan, I hadn't counted on enjoying it. Courtship and foreplay hadn't been considerations. It was a job, like a haunting or a boogie man eviction, and much like a haunting or a boogie man eviction, I dug the hell out of it, to the point I pulled off my shirt and threw it behind me. Screw it, this was a blast. If we stopped at the groping stage I was totally keen on going wherever the tingling took me.

I don't recall how I went from standing between his knees to on my back in his bed, but that's where I landed. He kissed me again, his hands skimming from my shoulders to my bra and over my stomach. I clenched my gut muscles partially because it tickled, partially because I didn't want him to find me all gelatinous and Stay Puft marshmallowy. He nosed at my cleavage, and then he giggled. Giggling from a 6'4" guy was bizarre, and I cracked an eye to determine what was so funny. Hopefully the sight of my partially clothed body wasn't point-and-laugh worthy, but if it was, I'd pretend his dong was a piñata.

"You're all soft. It's nice."

"... uhh. That's good. Right?"

"Nnnngh. Soft and warm."

"Yeeeeeep."

"You have a nice belly. I want to... I like your belly. Soft squishy girl belly."

I had no idea what to say to that. Of course, my brain immediately jumped to 'HE CALLED ME FAT' because of the squishy thing, but he kissed and nuzzled it so much that I couldn't muster an iota of real upset. I squirmed beneath him, and he took that for me liking it which, well—even drunk off his ass he could read the signs—and his hands fumbled with my jeans.

Oh hey. Houston, we have lift off.

THE INTRODUCTION OF lady parts into our antics—drunken and horny on his part, sober and quasi-horny on mine—

brought with it a new passel of worries. The primary one? What if he thought I looked WEIRD DOWN THERE. I was pretty sure everything worked the way it was supposed to work, but the only source material I had for this sort of thing was two minute internet porn clips and *The Miracle of Life* video from health class in junior high. That latter terrified me because stuff expanded and went all ovular when it should be smaller and watermelons out lemon-sized holes and...

I wasn't like that. I was pretty sure on that. I was not like that, and thanks to the condoms in my purse, I would not *be* like that for quite some time. If ever. Babies were tiny, cute crap machines, and if I wanted one of those, I'd get a puppy. At least you can give away a puppy if it annoys you.

Ian grunted again, this time because he couldn't get my underwear past my hips without me lifting my butt. I had no idea where my jeans were, though my shirt glowed on the floor thanks to its white pinstripes, and I stared at it as his hands skimmed from my ankles to my knees and thighs. I lifted up, swallowing a slightly panicked yelp when I felt him getting closer and closer to what was surely *ugly, weird, and malformed, and OH MY GOD WHAT THE HELL WAS I DOING?!*

The good news was, on the off chance I was a freakish anomaly with the strangest looking pants bits in the world, Ian either didn't care or he was too drunk to notice. His cheek pressed against my stomach as he touched me. It was weird at first, weird enough that I almost chickened out and told him I couldn't do it, but that wouldn't accomplish anything except leave him with a boner and me with a whole lot of self-loathing. Ninety percent of the women in the world had been or would be in the same place I was.

People had been having The Sex since the beginning of time, and they would continue doing so right up until the sun died and took Earth with it.

It was okay. I'd be fine.

For some reason, thinking those things made me feel better. Admitting that *it was okay to be nervous* made me feel better, too. I was probably the only remaining virgin among all of the girls at the party, which meant every single one of them had gone through a similar experience and survived. I was infinitely cooler than they were, and so much more bad-ass it wasn't even funny. If those chicks could get laid without it becoming a catastrophic freak-out, so could I.

There was only one problem.

"Whoa, dude. It's not your enemy. Holy shit." Ian's touching had turned to pawing, and pawing apparently meant strangling my most sensitive part like he hated it and wanted to punish it forever. His finger stabbed at it like a battering ram laying siege to a castle door.

"Huh? Are you okay, Maggie?" He looked up, his hand stilling. I forced a winning smile. In the black light, winning smile meant 'smear of evil glowing fangs' but there wasn't much I could do about that.

"Yeah, it's cool."

"Sorry. Do you want me to stop?"

"No!" I practically yelled it into his face, but there was no way I psyched myself up this much to have the whole thing fizzle out. By the way he recoiled, I knew I'd been too emphatic, and I ran my hands over his shoulders, bunching the cloth of his jersey up in my fists. "No please don't. It's okay," I said, trying for soothing when I wanted to scream at him to do it already, I was losing my nerve. He nodded and lifted his arms, letting me pull off his shirt. I could barely make out the number tattooed on his shoulder, a big, blocky 58, before he moved up over me, tongue sliding from my stomach to the valley between my boobs and then to my neck. "I like you. Okay?" He whispered against my ear, slurring worse than ever. I turned my face to kiss his cheek mostly to keep myself from saying anything stupid.

Get it done, I said to myself. *Shut up and get it done.*

"You're okay, Maggie?" He said, and I realized he expected me to answer. This wasn't drunken rhetoric.

"... yeah. I'm okay. I like you, too."

"Cool." I heard him fumble with his belt, and was about to offer him a condom from my purse, but he pulled open the drawer of his nightstand and got one of his own. He shifted, there was a snapping sound, and I braced below him, going rigid in anticipation of... well. Sex. I guess I figured he'd ravage me like some rutting tribal beast. If the way he'd pawed me was any indication, he assumed his penis was the Hatfields, and my vagina was the McCoys, and we were at war. It didn't bode well for the actual deed.

The truth was, he was gentle, and slid a tiny bit inside of me as he rained kisses over my ear. I closed my eyes and forced myself to relax, sweeping the tips of my fingers over his shoulders and upper back for encouragement. He liked that and murmured, going deeper, moving over to capture my mouth in a kiss that, under any other circumstance, would have been sweet.

For a moment, I believed it was good, that everything was good and we'd be okay, that I'd done all right by finding Ian and tomorrow I'd be a journeyman hunter.

And then he collapsed on top of me, totally passed out.

CHAPTER FIVE

I DIDN'T KNOW if I should laugh, cry, or put Ian in a sleeper hold. No, he *already* slept, that'd exacerbate the problem. I shoved his shoulder, at first to see if I could get him to wake up and finish—he was clearly capable by the feel of things—but when that proved futile, it was to get him off of me. I only half-managed the second, oozing out from under his weight so he sprawled across my right side. I stared at the wall, incredulous that what should be a simple thing had somehow managed to go so wrong.

I wasn't sure what I should do with myself then. Julie'd been drinking, and she told me when we made the plans that we'd be staying overnight. I wasn't such an ass that I'd ask her to risk a DUI so I could sulk in the comfort of my home. I supposed I could socialize with other people, maybe salvage something decent out of my failed hookup, but being the lone sober person in a nest of drunken idiots wasn't my idea of a good time.

Screw it, I was going to bed.

I wriggled out from under Ian to slide under his blankets, uncaring that I hogged both them and the pillows. It was his penance for failing to properly hump me. I hoped he got frostbite on his butt crack, or at the very least slept poorly because he was cold. I growled as I pounded on his pillow and rolled over, away from him, willing the sweet oblivion of sleep to distance me from what happened.

Falling asleep quickly was a relief and a surprise. I had a hard time with it whenever my mother wasn't around. A stupid thing to admit considering how old I was, but we'd moved around a lot when I was a kid. We didn't go far, mostly bouncing from one house to another in the same town so she could maintain her hunting territory, but that didn't mean I didn't know a lot of different beds over the years. Mom was my onc stable thing—my fleshy night light.

That didn't stop me from drooling my dreams into Ian's bed like it was the most natural thing in the world. Maybe it was having a body right there beside me. He'd be a pretty big human shield if something went bad, and I wasn't such a peach I wouldn't hide behind a veritable stranger to save my hide. Or maybe it was that people who didn't seek out monsters didn't have to deal with them. Everyone knows monsters exist, of course, and are aware of the dangers they *can* present, but monsters keep to themselves. If they didn't, the DoPR (and by association the hunters) would be after them. Terrorizing norms flew in the face of a very basic self-preservation tenet.

Whatever the case, I slept like a fat drunken baby, waking up feeling pretty good in spite of the previous night's antics. I tried rolling over to get out of bed, but a long wiry arm held me tight, anchored around my waist. A bare leg, all furry and full of boy cooties, rested between my calves.

"Wake up. I need to leave," I said, deciding I no longer needed to be polite. Ian failed his quest to do me, and that meant instead of impressing him, I could be more of an ass. Well, more me-like anyway, which tended to be ass-like.

His answer was to mumble and nuzzle at the back of my neck.

"No, really. I have to pee. I could pee in your bed if you want."

It was amazing how the threat of rampant urination got people moving. "Don't have to scream, Melissa. M'right here."

My breath caught in my throat. I shouldn't have cared that he'd called me his ex-girlfriend's name. It wasn't like I hadn't used him, or tried to use him, when he was drunk and vulnerable after a break up. Of course, he'd climbed into bed with the first girl that threw herself at him, so that didn't make him a champion of all that was rainbows and unicorn sparkles, either.

"Maggie."

"Mag... oh shit. Right. I... shit. I'm sorry." He lurched upright behind me. I craned my head over my shoulder to peer at him. He looked like he'd been shot at and missed, shit at and hit. His carefully-gelled spikes were limp atop his head. Plum-colored circles shadowed his eyes, his skin washed out and sickly green. "I'm really... really sorry. Like, I don't... I usually don't do this so..."

"I bet you say that to all the girls." I scooted down to the foot of his bed to search for my panties. Somehow, they'd ended up hanging from the front of his dresser, and I snagged them from the knob, wiggling into them as discretely as possible.

"No. I don't fuck people I don't know. I've only... there was only Melissa so I... "

"You don't owe me any explanations." I grabbed my pants from the floor and tugged them on, uncaring that I was pointed butt first in his direction. After someone's played around with your no-no parts, ass shots didn't seem like such a big deal anymore. "And we didn't fuck so much as pretend we were going to and then you passed out on me, so... yeah."

It was cruel to say it like that, and by his near-pathetic groan, I knew I'd struck a nerve. It's what I'd wanted, to let him know exactly how badly he failed me, so then why did I feel like such a dick for saying it? "Sorry. I more mean it's cool, we didn't get that far so you're off the hook."

"I don't want to be off the hook. This sucks."

He watched me shrug into my shirt, a frown pasted across his mouth. I paid no attention to the buttons and thus misaligned the sides, but by the time I noticed I'd ventured into wardrobe malfunction territory, I couldn't bring myself to care. It felt weird in here now, awkward and tense, and I wanted to rouse Julie so I could go home. The sooner I could put this mini-disaster behind me, the better.

"You know, we should hang some time. Like, go out for reals, you know? You can give me your number and... "

"I don't have a phone," I said. He made another gurgling groany noise, and again I felt like a jerk. I sighed and approached his mirror, licking my thumb to dab at the mascara smudges under my eyes. I wanted to play it cool, distant and chill like I was a frost queen, but I couldn't stop myself from stealing a glance at him in our shared reflection. He stared at my back, looking lost and sad, and though I liked to play at being a hard-hearted bitch from Hell, the truth was...

The truth was nothing. I *am* a hard-hearted bitch from Hell, damn it. Ian... well, he sparked something different in me. For seven whole seconds he exposed my creamy, nougat center.

"Look, why don't you give me your number? We just moved, so I can call you when I get set up."

Another one of Janice's spectacular life lessons: lying is fine as long as A) you don't get caught and B) when you do get caught you're a big enough person to admit it. I'd worry about the consequences of my lies if and only if I ventured into B territory. Until then, all bets were off.

"Cool. Okay cool. We can hang or whatevs."

He scribbled a number onto the back of a receipt and held it out. I snatched it without looking at him, stuffing my feet into my shoes and double-timing it for the door.

"Fun party," I said before disappearing down the hall.

"Yeah, thanks for... "

I didn't hear the end of that sentence. I was too busy running away.

DOWNSTAIRS WAS A post-apocalyptic war zone, complete with bodies littering the ground and a weird funk on the air. I picked my way around the carnage to find Julie, who slept on top of some guy I'd never seen before. At least she'd gotten couch space; squishy furniture was prime real estate when there were thirty-something kids clamoring for a place to crash.

I poked her in the shoulder to wake her. She lifted her head and smiled, sweeping her hair out of her eyes. I hated her for how good she already looked, no effort required, like being gorgeous was something she did for fun on Saturdays. I wasn't hung up on my appearance for the most part, but there was something about Julie that made me feel 'less', like she was the embodiment of feminine charm while all I had to show for my girl-hood was a pair of boobs and a year's supply of Tampax in my linen closet. Of course, my answer to feeling sub-par was to hit something, which wasn't exactly girly either, so I couldn't win for losing.

Julie extricated herself from the man-mattress beneath her to wander to the bathroom, taking her sweet time re-emerging. At least the wait was worth it; she had her purse in hand and looked ready to leave. I'd been ready for that for about ten hours.

"How'd things go with Ian?"

"He's uhh. He's nice."

She peered at me like I was supposed to elaborate, but that was all I could muster. "Yeah, thanks for letting me near-boff your cousin" didn't sound right, and I wasn't one to spew my private life stuff all over the place. Not unless I had to.

When she figured out I had zero intention of spilling, she headed for the stairs. "He is. A nice guy I mean. I knew you'd like him. I dunno, it seems a good fit. I'm gonna go say bye then we can hit the road, 'kay?"

I watched her take the steps two at a time, idly hoping Ian had thought to put on some pants after I left. If not, she'd jump to a whole slew of conclusions right off the bat. None of them would be wrong conclusions, but it was the principle of the thing. I didn't want to kiss and tell.

Or quasi-hump and tell. Whatever.

A chorus of dry heaves echoed around me as teenagers tore themselves from their drunken reveries. One girl combatant crawled across the floor towards the bathroom, positively green. I put my back against the wall to keep myself out of frontal-cone spew range. A kid in the kitchen moved some dishes aside so he could puke in the sink. I hadn't had more than a sip to drink, but I felt sick by association. I slunk outside and sat on the front step, glad Julie'd been smart enough to park on the street instead of in the driveway. This way we wouldn't have to do the call out of WHOEVER DRIVES THE BLACK TRUCK AND THE WHITE CONVERTIBLE, CAN YOU MOVE? Those people were barely capable of amoeba-scale function. The driveway shuffle was way beyond them.

A few minutes later, Julie joined me, a pair of oversized, diva sunglasses perched on her nose.

"What are you doing tomorrow night?"

"Not sure. I'd have to check with Mom. Why?"

"How is Janice?"

It should have weirded me out that Julie called my mom by her first name, but Mom insisted that Miss or Mrs. made her feel old, and anyone caught calling her that would get a Wet Willy. It had been like Pavlov's dog after that; as no one liked having a wet finger wedged up their ear, they fell in line quickly. "Good. She had a hunt last night."

"Cool! I'm surprised you came out. You love that stuff, you freak."

"Well, yeah, but I can't do werewolf jobs yet. They're too high up the chain for a newb like me." An opportunity for me to confess I tried to molest her cousin for a job promotion, and yet, I refrained. It's like I wanted to maintain my singular friendship.

"Cool. So, tomorrow night, if you're not doing anything, you should come hang. I'm going out with Ian's friend John, and the four of us could hit food. Ian sounded down."

An orthodontist appointment sounded more fun than going out with Ian, but I put on my best game face and nodded. Telling Julie her cousin was a limp-weenied failure wouldn't go over big. "Maybe. I'll call you. It depends on the workload."

"You should. You guys would work. His ex-girlfriend was a massive bitch, so I think you'd be good for him."

"Because I'm a massive bitch, too, or..."

"No! Because I like you, and he needs to date someone I can stand for once. His girlfriends are terribad. And I'd get to see you more, too, which'd be cool."

"Yeah."

She maintained her chatter all the way to my house, though I can't tell you a single thing that was said. I was way too preoccupied wrestling with my guilt. Maybe I didn't screw up a lot in general and thus didn't have to deal with guilt, or maybe I'd become an expert at justifying whatever terrible thing I'd done at any given time, but the Ian situation bugged me. If he'd been a dismissive dick about it, everything would have been fine, but no. He'd been nice and apologetic the morning after, and that meant my rampant snark was...

Wrong. It was wrong. It was like kicking a kitten. Who did that? Who kicked a kitten for fun?

Maggie Cunningham, that's who.

Man, I suck.

BY THE TIME my mother came home from her overnight venture, I'd been wallowing in self-loathing for well over three hours. I was pantsless, there was a half-eaten bag of Ranch Doritos on the couch seat beside me, and the Oprah Network was on TV. There was no sadder sight than a seventeen-year-old girl watching a bunch of fifty-something women talk about hot-flashes, randomly leaking nipples, and the emotional challenges of menopause.

Mom dropped her gear in the foyer, the weapons, armor, and other hunting sundries making a racket as they struck the tile. "Whoa. You look rough. Don't tell me you stayed in last night?"

"Nope."

"What'd you end up doing?"

"Went to a party and got laid. Well, tried to get laid. Funny story, that."

"Oh, yeah? Use a condom?"

I gritted my teeth and shut off the television, fixing my eyes on the dead, black screen in front of me. "You realize it's totally screwed up that you're fine with me finding a piece of random ass, right? You *should* be going on some spiel about self-respect right now."

"Why's that?"

"I dunno. Most mothers would."

"Well, then most mothers think sex is shameful for a woman and I think that's a heaping pile of shit. As long as you're okay and your boy treated you right, no spiel. If he treated you bad, I'll cram his dick down his throat and watch him choke." She threw herself onto the couch next to me, and I got my first good look at the claw marks raking her face. Four gouges marred her cheek, crusts of dried blood and dirt mucking up the edges, the thickest one in the middle split so wide I wondered if she needed stitches.

"Oh my God. What happened?" I stared at the injury, feeling faint that the top part of the longest cut was less than an inch from her eye.

"Werewolf. Help me clean it in a few? Not yet, though. Kinda want to sit around and eat Doritos with my daughter for a minute. Unless she's going to be a bitch and pick a fight because she's in a bad mood, in which case I'll go eat Doritos in the kitchen and have a beer."

I twitched. She was right. This was the second person I'd taken my bad mood out on today, and she was the second person who didn't deserve it. Well, Ian kind of did, but not totally. "Sorry. Point taken."

"Good. So what do you mean 'tried' to get laid. That sounds ominous." She crunched on a Dorito and offered me the bag, like I wasn't responsible for half of it being empty already.

I waved her off. "Well, he got kinda in and then passed out so I dunno if it counts. I mean, it was flesh in flesh but... ya know. That was it."

"... how'd he..."

"Drunk."

"Ouch. Sorry to hear it. That's not on you, okay? Nothing to do with you."

I listened to her crunch on chips, thinking about Julie's offer to go out tomorrow night and whether or not I wanted to take her up on it. The idea of a date with a guy who'd only be going out with me because of some sense of duty bugged me. He was still into his ex if he called me by her name, and that didn't lend itself to happily-ever-after. I supposed I could go on the off chance that we'd get more alone time, and maybe he'd take care of the questionable state of my virginity, but did I want to put either of us through that again? He was Julie's cousin and I liked Julie. I wanted her to like me the next time I talked to her.

I must have looked miserable because Mom slung her arm over my shoulder and gave me a squeeze. "It happens. I'm sorry it happened to you. Look, I'll cut you a deal. Let's get my face cleaned up, and later when it gets dark, we'll park up the street from Plasma. If someone comes sniffing around, we'll know whether or not we can do a vamp job, okay?"

Plasma was the local vamp bar, and vamp bars were loaded with fledgling bloodsuckers looking to show off their powers. For newbie fangers, it was a great place to get a snack and a lay. The old ones had too much dignity to be seen in such poorly-lit clichés. Their progeny, though, not so much. They flocked to them, dressed in their tight patent leather and fishnet shirts, calling their style 'goth chic' which translated to 'poser douches.' But, hey, truth in advertising for once. At least we knew where to go if we wanted a spaz-out for virgin blood.

"That sounds awesome. Thanks, Mom."

AN HOUR LATER, I had my mother handcuffed to a kitchen chair, her ankles strapped to the legs with a pair of bungee cords. Her good cheek lay flat on the dining table, and she gripped a belt between her teeth in case. I'd positioned my body in such a way that, when necessary, I could lunge on top of her and hold her down.

This was gonna blow.

Injuries sustained while hunting were always bad news, but nothing was worse than monster claws or fangs because on top of the normal damage, they tainted the wound. It was better to be slammed upside the head by a monster holding a crowbar than it was to be directly attacked by them, or in the case of my mother, cut by them. It was like being hit with a hypodermic needle; whatever the monster had, you had now too, except instead of disease you got their curse. No, that didn't mean Mom would grow furry—she'd have to be bitten on a full moon for that—but it did mean if we left the scrapes unattended, they'd fester and never close. It was worse with vampire wounds. If they DNA'd all over you, they could find you later, like their curse magically tagged you. That was a fast track way to having your insides become your outsides.

"Okay, you ready?" I asked, dunking a facecloth into a bowl of holy water. I got it good and wet, saturating the cloth without bothering to wring it out. Mom jerked her head in a nod and closed her eyes, her shoulders stiff. I took that as my invitation to finish. "Okay. I'm going to count to three. One... "

I didn't get to two. I slapped the facecloth against her cheek and jumped on top of her, pinning her to the table. Mom thrashed beneath me, screaming and bucking so much the chair came up off of the floor and slammed back down again in a series of squealing rattles. Her head nailed me in the gut, forcing the air out of my middle, but I held tight, thinking this was how a rodeo cowboy felt on top of a bucking bronco.

Mom once described getting cleansed like holding your hand in a pot of boiling water—that it burned and throbbed so badly you'd do anything to get away from the pain. I believed it; the last time I helped her with a tainted wound, she acted like I'd tried to kill her. We'd wrestled around like a pair of cats until I sat on her butt and pinned her arms, giving up on the facecloth and pouring the bowl of holy water all over her head. We tried avoiding similar hysterics this time around with the handcuffs and bungees. It worked. I couldn't breathe, and I was fairly sure if I stayed on top of her for too much longer she'd suffocate beneath me, but at least she'd stayed in one place.

Progress. Ish.

She went slack, her struggles petering out in a series of pained mewls. I took that as my cue to climb off her, and I wriggled back 'til my feet touched the ground. The moment I looked at her, I felt like the worst daughter in the universe. Her face was so red it was almost purple, and her eyes leaked rivers of tears. The cuts were stark white, the holy water burning the taint from them and bleaching them in the process.

"That was fun," she rasped, spitting the belt out onto the floor. "Should do it again sometime."

I unlocked the handcuffs. "Sorry."

"Had to be done." Angry, red chafe marks encircled her wrists, and she rubbed at them while I worked the bungees off her ankles. "Might as well do the silver now, too."

She grabbed a teaspoon from the table and bopped me on the forehead with it, a tight smile playing around her mouth. I snagged it from her with a smirk. If the holy water hadn't purified a part of the wound, the silver would, and I ran the curved bottom of the spoon over each cut, careful to get under the flaps of torn flesh. She yelped when the silver made contact with residual flecks of taint, but it was nowhere near as bad as the holy water cleansing. I only had to grip her jaw once to hold her in place.

"That's it," I announced, eyeballing my work. I was pretty sure the thickest of the cuts would leave a scar—even purified it had an unsightly gape quality—but the rest of them had shriveled up tight, the ends puckering together like a days-old injury instead of a fresh one.

"Just think, one day I'll be holding you down to fix your cuts. Won't that be fun? A real mother-daughter bonding experience." She picked up the cuffs to jingle them at me. "Literally."

"Right. Last night taught me I'm going to be an apprentice for the rest of my life."

"Booze is a cock-killer, Margaret, but it's not the end of the world. It'll happen. Remember it's not your fault, okay?"

"I know it's not."

"Good. I'm going to hit the shower then. After that, dinner and Plasma, yeah?" She ruffled my hair like I was seven before making her way towards the bathroom. She stopped to turn on the stereo on her way. I watched her rifle through her CDs, pushing one into the player. A minute later Grace Slick's questionably melodic voice talked about one pill making me larger, and another making me smaller. Mom shout-sang along, tugging her shirt off and throwing it onto the floor.

I followed in her wake, picking up her laundry and stuffing it into the hamper in the hall. Life'd never be dull so long as I raised my mother.

CHAPTER SIX

MOM OFTEN WONDERED why the van reeked like dirty people armpits—her words, not mine. She'd comment on it here and there, more as an 'out loud thought to herself' than an actual question. I generally ignored it, but today, watching her eat a nasty pile of sludgy looking food, I couldn't resist poking her.

"Fish tacos. That's why."

She bit into a crunchy taco shell. "Huh?"

"Fish tacos. You want to know why it stinks in here? You eat gross food. Fish tacos are gross food."

"Mmmm. Delicious fish tacos," she said, offering me a bite. I shrank into my seat, putting my hand up as if to ward off a blow. The taco had pink fish meat swimming in a sea of guacamole. It looked like an Area 51 experiment gone wrong, and there was *no way* it belonged in my mouth.

"Get that out of my face."

"It's good for you, Margaret Jane. Fish is brain food."

"It's nasty looking! And it's Maggie. Ugh. I want to punch you sometimes."

"MWAH."

We'd parked three blocks up the street from Plasma. Mom considered it a safe enough distance. Her fear was, if I was still mystically tagged as the big V, we wouldn't get *one* fledgling vampire on a rampage, we'd get *many*. She'd taken down some old, powerful fangers over the years, but that was with daylight on her side and seasoned hunters backing her up. She'd taught me lots about killing monsters, but I was too green to be considered reliable. She had to approach this like she was on her own.

I wasn't totally useless, though. My wrists were strapped with silver blades, I had a wooden stake across my lap, and there was a bucket of water balloons behind me. I'd specifically chosen the pale pink ones first, followed by the lavender and white ones. If I'd be hurling Molotov cocktail holy bombs at attacking vamps, I wanted them to be in pretty pastel colors. Because that was funny to me. Because I wasn't right in the head.

"So how do they deal with a virgin that's stupid enough to walk into the fanger bar?"

"They're not allowed in," Mom said, stuffing her taco mess into a bag and throwing it in the back. She laid her crossbow over her lap and popped the seat back so she could recline. "The bouncers work two ways at Plasma. They keep virgins out, and keep the baby fangs from going berserk. Plus a lot of the little ones have handlers."

I'd heard of handlers before. They were more experienced vamps who palled around with initiates to keep them out of trouble, like a Big Brothers, Big Sisters program for the undead. DoPR had a very baseball approach to monsters: three strikes and you were out. Three separate incidents of violence against a norm, an agency would be contacted to hunt your ass. Extreme violence could get a hunter on you right away, no previous offenses needed. A responsible sire, meaning the big daddy vampire who bestowed his gift to the mini-vamp, would employ a handler to babysit his offspring so he could go do whatever it was old vampires did—being aloof or buying couture fashion or some crap—while someone else got to deal with all of the ugly, boring stuff. Ugly, boring stuff included keeping the fanglets from sinking teeth into an unsuspecting innocent.

"So tell me about the guy," Mom said.

"What guy?"

"THE guy."

"Ian? Oh. He's tall. Uh. Dark hair."

"And?"

"And what, he's Julie's cousin. She wants me to go out with them and some dude named John tomorrow."

"You gonna go?" Mom sat up straighter, her eyes narrowing as she peered up the sidewalk. It wasn't quite sundown yet, but the skies had gone that mulled cider gold of late day. Vamps would be venturing out any time now. Mom hoped to pique the interest of an early riser before it fed so it'd be weaker and easier to fend off. I followed her gaze and immediately spotted the vampire. She was short and squat, shaped like a pumpkin though she tried to hide her roundness by layering her lace and pleather. The clothes weren't the giveaway to her lack of pulse, though. That was her pallor. She hadn't seen sunlight in a while, and it gave her naturally-darker skin an ashen quality.

She looked our way for only a minute, but then ducked into the Plasma parking lot. I exhaled and sank back into my seat. "I don't know. If I'm going, I mean. It's not like I have anything in common with him. When I met him, he was trashed."

"So you don't know if you *don't* have anything in common with him either. You must have seen something in him if you let him put his winky in you." She grinned and pulled out her cigarette gum, popping a piece into her mouth.

"You're gross. What I saw in him was the fact he was male and available."

"So? You should go! See if you like him. My one regret being a hunter is I don't do more normal people shit. Dates are fun and I'm all about fun. Besides, if you wimp out I'll have to rag on you for the rest of your life."

Considering what a pain my mother was on a normal day, her amping it up to prod me about Ian sounded excruciatingly annoying. "Fiiiiine." I pulled out my phone, trying to remember Julie's number. Since I only called her once a month, I didn't have it memorized, but what I did have was my purse, and my purse had the receipt with Ian's number on it. I picked up the pocketbook, dangling the strap off of my fingertip like handling it too long would disease me.

"Something wrong?"

"No. Just feels weird calling a guy who called me his ex-girlfriend's name oh..." I glanced at the clock on the van stereo. "Ten hours ago."

Mom scowled. "You didn't mention that. Was he wasted?"

"Yeah."

"Eh. Might have been a fluke. Only way to find out is to... fill in the rest of the sentence here."

I filled it in by finding the receipt and dialing. Mom watched me, an awful grin plastered across her face. Not only did I have to deal with the choke-worthy reality of talking to Ian, but I had to worry that my mother would do something Janice-like and embarrass me while I talked to him. "What are you going..."

"Hey."

Ian's voice stopped me cold, and I licked my lips, sucking in a breath that probably made him think I was a mouth breather. I hated mouth breathers; I always pictured them shaped like the Death Star and stinking like Cheetos. "Hey. It's Maggie."

"'Sup?"

So we were back to "'sup"ing. I didn't know how to answer it this time around, but I wouldn't sweat it either. If he wanted to be uncommunicative, that was his prerogative, but I refused to work twice as hard to make conversation happen. If that's what he expected from me, he could take a dump in his hat.

"Julie said something about hanging tomorrow night." My eyes drifted to my mom and she winked at me, stuffing another piece of gum into her maw. "Didn't know if you were game or not."

"Oh, yeah. Cool."

That's it? That's all you've got for me?

I went quiet, embracing the awkward silence spreading between us. If something else had to be said, it was on him. Otherwise I'd linger on the phone line 'til he got sick of me and hung up. Let him call me a creepy stalker chick. I didn't care. I'd been called far worse by my mother this week alone; when I didn't put the dishes away after dinner on Wednesday she'd called me a pimple on the ass of humanity.

Surprisingly, Ian rose to the occasion. He took a deep breath, stammered for a few seconds, and I realized he was nervous. Was Ian *shy*? I'd heard this word 'shy' before, but its meaning, it did not compute. 'Shy' was like dinosaurs or the dodo bird—a thing I knew existed, but had never experienced firsthand. "Can I pick you up? Might be good to, like, talk alone first."

I smiled for some inane reason. Mom noticed it, too, jabbing me in the side with a pointy finger. "Sure. What time?"

"Seven?"

I gave him my address and listened as he fumbled for a pen.

"Cool," he said. "I'll see you tomorrow. Hey can I—" He cleared his throat, and I swung my eyes to the van roof as I waited for him to assemble the thought. "—are you a hunter? Julie said. Well, she said."

Screw you, Julie. That wasn't your news to tell.

"Yeah. My mom is, and I'm a fourth year. Hope that's not a problem."

"Not at all. It's cool."

"It is?"

I was cool? This was news to me. Wait, no, that's not right. Yes. I was cool. Yes, I knew this. I was awesome. Maggie Cunningham, The Awesome. Everyone should want my autograph.

"Yeah."

"Sweet. Well, I gotta go. We're out at a vampire thing now so…" My eyes strayed to my mother and she smirked before holding up her hands, making a circle with the pointer and thumb of one hand while poking a finger through it over and over with the other. I smacked at her wrist, then slammed my fist down on her upper thigh, trying to give her a charley horse. She cackled like the Wicked Witch. "Yeah, I gotta go."

"Cool. See you tomorrow, Maggie."

"Later."

When I hung up, I hit Mom's thigh over and over, looking for the sweet spot to cause a cramp.

"You bitch!" She shoved back at me, darting a hand in to give me the world's worst titty twister. I howled aloud, shriek-laughing as I climbed from my side of the van to hers. We were so busy squabbling we didn't notice the vampire rapidly approaching from my side of the car. In fact, we didn't notice it 'til its hand punched through the passenger side glass to fist in my sweatshirt, yanking me backward.

"DOWN, MAGGIE. GET DOWN."

When Mom had that tone, it brooked no argument. I tried to drop. Unfortunately, the fang had me in such a way that down didn't *work*. It lurched its arm up, and I went with it, slamming my head into the roof of the van. It hurt, but not nearly as much as the shards of glass shredding through my sweatshirt to rip into my back fat, sending white hot pain sizzling down my spine.

I knew I shoulda lost those thirty pounds sooner.

"Shiiiiit!"

I reached for my mother, but she did one better and stuffed a water balloon at me. My brain cramped, not registering what I was supposed to do, but as soon as I figured it out, I lifted the balloon over my head and squeezed, breaking it over myself and the vamp holding onto me. It howled before relinquishing its hold, sending me sprawling over my car seat. Holy water dribbled down my shoulders, but something warmer and thicker dribbled down my sides. Blood.

Mom took the opportunity to launch a silver-tipped arrow through the broken window, which was met with a shriek. I lifted my gaze to look at my attacker, getting my first look at a frenzying vampire. The she-fang's eyes were bloodshot and wide. A series of bulging veins stuck out at her temples and along the column of her throat, like one of those muscle-men you saw dragging eighteen-wheelers for competition on TV. Her mouth gaped open, far too many fangs gleaming white in my direction. Mom always said vampires had more than the two long incisors—that the movies got it wrong. She'd understated by a lot; this was more like piranha teeth, rows of sharp jags pointed out at odd angles. If they bit you, there'd be no polite side-by-side puncture wounds. There'd be gashes and pieces of flesh missing.

Another one of Mom's arrows took the vampire in the shoulder. She staggered back, screeching, rabid in her fury and need for a Maggie-snack. But before she could regain her bearings and lunge for me again, a second vampire appeared. He wrapped his arms around her to haul her away. My attacker didn't like that. Her heels raked over the pavement, her head thrashing back and forth as she jerked and writhed.

A *handler*, I thought to myself, thankful for the second vampire's brute strength. The first vampire used her claws to shred at him, tearing his shirt apart and digging bloody furrows into his forearms, but he took it all in stride, lifting her off of the ground like she weighed nothing at all.

"Stop, Lizzie."

"I'll kill you. I'll fucking hunt you down and kill you!" She spit at me. "I'll drain you!"

Mom kept one arm up, holding the crossbow, while the other put the key into the ignition. The engine roared to life. Mom handed me the weapon. As soon as I had a grip, she peeled off the curb and tore down the street, her hands locked at the ten and two position, knuckles white where they throttled the wheel.

"How bad are you hurt?"

"I'm bleeding," I said, not sure what else to say.

"Claws or glass or what?"

"Glass, I think. I couldn't see it, but it hurts."

"Fuck."

I wasn't sure if she was bemoaning my injury, or the fact that we weren't all that far away from the vampire and the street light in front of us turned red. A steady stream of two-lane traffic forced us to stop at the intersection. Mom's eyes flicked to the rear view, watching like she expected the vampire to gnaw our back bumper. She wasn't all that far off the mark. Screams erupted from the street behind us. It was a terrible sound—a baying, shrill thing that made me wince, my hold tightening on the crossbow. It got closer and closer as the fang barreled our way. My eyes swung to my mirror, waiting for the blur of motion that would herald the vampire's arrival.

Yes, vampires appear in mirrors. Books and movies screw up a lot of the finer details.

"Hold tight," Mom said. I had enough time to brace a leg against the dash before Mom jerked the van into reverse and put the pedal to the floor. We careened backwards, propelled as if launched from a cannon. I let out a startled shriek, unsure of what the hell was going on. Then there was a thud and another scream as we hit something solid. Mom stopped, put the car into drive, went forward a few feet, and then went into reverse again, hitting that same lump over.

And over. And over.

"Bitch wants to threaten my kid? Let her eat grit." Mom snagged the crossbow from me and got out of the car, loading another arrow as she moved. Despite my terror, I followed, my legs quivering like Jell-O. My mother'd run over someone to keep me safe. It seemed stupid to let her finish it without me despite every instinct I had telling me to *run and hide and get away now.*

The smears along the pavement stretched for twenty or thirty feet. Viscera covered the road, puddles of blood and gore soiling the asphalt. Nothing should have survived a trauma like that, yet the vampire gurgled like her guts weren't strewn all over. That her middle was flattened and divided in half hadn't caught up to her brain.

"Sometimes the best thing to do is to cut your losses," Mom announced in her 'I'm giving you a lesson so pay attention' voice. She raised the crossbow. "When they're too far gone to back down, when all they see is meat, we end them. Period. No second chances."

"Wait!"

A man's voice, the handler's voice, tore our attention away from the shuddering meat pile. He stood there with his torn shirt and shredded arms, fists balled at his side. At first I thought he was angry, like he held himself back from attacking us for hurting her, but then I noticed how his shoulders trembled, the way his tongue slicked over his lips. He wasn't mad, he was *scared.* "Her sire will pay. He'll pay well. She's young and inexperienced. Let her go. Please."

"Why'd *you* let her go, dipshit?"

"She said she was fine. She said she needed a drink. I thought..."

"You thought wrong." Mom fired an arrow into the fledgling's head. Whatever you may have heard about vampires needing to be staked and beheaded and 'that's the only way to kill them' is crap. Silver works wonders on them, too, a noxious poison that collapses their veins when put somewhere important, like brains or hearts. The vampire's screams cut short, her mouth falling open as white, foamy spittle pooled at the corners of her lips. Her ravaged body shuddered—even the parts separated from her torso—and then it went still, collapsing with a squish.

"Get a couple balloons," Mom said. "Head and neck. I'll stake the heart for good measure and phone this into the clean-up crew."

"Okay." I did as I was told, trying not to stare too long at any one gob of vampire flesh as I holy watered the corpse. The dead flesh fizzled and smoked, filling the air with a distinctly bacon-y smell. It did nothing for my queasy stomach.

" No. Why?" The handler ran his hand over his face. "How... why? She was helpless. You didn't have to kill her."

Mom snorted. "Helpless? My ass. I'm a federally registered hunter, and your charge threatened me and my partner not once, but twice. The moment she came after us a second time, it was over. Don't like it, talk to the DoPR."

"But... " The handler went to his knees before the biggest pile of fanger goo. "But she was an elder's first born. This can't happen."

That gave my mother pause, though if you didn't know her you wouldn't be able to tell—a slight tension around her eyes, crow's feet where there normally weren't any. She collected herself quickly, shrugging her shoulders and heading back to the van. "He can make another."

"Not another first born."

"Sucks to be him then, don't it?"

CHAPTER SEVEN

I STRADDLED THE toilet in the bathroom, my sweatshirt cut open from shoulders to waist, my bra hanging off my biceps. Mom didn't want me lifting my arms because she didn't want me to unclot, so she dismantled my outfit with a pocket knife and a pair of scissors.

"Well, there's good news and there's bad news."

"Bad news first."

"You're the Big V. I'm afraid you'll have to deal with penis again." I stared at the wall in front of me, finding Mom's attempt at humor lacking, all things considered. Pancaking an elder's first progeny was a punch to the ovaries; there was no way the elder would take it well, and an eye witness meant our involvement couldn't go ignored. The handler probably painted us as whores of Babylon to a butthurt, powerful superior.

Not good.

Mom peeled the sweatshirt away to run a damp cloth over my cut. "The good news is I hit you with holy water and you're not screaming. It's not a vamp tag. I'm going to clean you and super-glue you to be sure, but you should be good to go."

"Super glue me?"

"Yeah. I don't think you need stitches, but we'll glue you shut in case." I wouldn't ask. Mom had been performing first aid on herself since she started hunting with my grandparents twenty years ago. The only time she *hadn't* mended her own cuts and bruises was the year she took off to be pregnant with me. If she said I needed to be glued, glued I would be.

She prodded the tender, broken flesh of my cut, and though I swore I wouldn't cry, my eyes welled up anyway. It stung. Mom couldn't see me, but she must have been able to tell I wanted to snivel like an infant because she made conversation to distract me. "If that vampire was an elder's first child, we might have some complications. The elders tend not to bite any old meat sack. She might have been someone, you know, important."

"So we're moving again," I said, used to this routine. Any time Mom thought a monster might come after her, we relocated to stay one step ahead.

"Not necessarily. It's always a possibility with this business, but the ball's in the elder's court now. He might take it out on the handler's ass for being a moron and letting her go at us a second time. It's not like we hid that we were hunters."

Mom reached for something in the medicine cabinet. I kept my eyes fixed on the wallpaper in front of me, following the printed ivy pattern as it twisted its way toward the ceiling. She poked and squeezed, I cringed and swallowed my whimpers. I was tough, damn it, even if my nerve endings demanded I curl in a corner and thrash like I'd diddled an electrical socket.

Eventually, something cold touched my skin followed by a flat, steady pressure as Mom put her palm against my back to hold the skin together.

"Promise me something?"

"What?"

"You'll go on that date tomorrow, and before you get all pissy-pants over the suggestion, listen to me, Margaret Jane." She pulled away her hand to sit on the edge of the tub, peering at me from beneath her too-plucked eyebrows. I sniffled, wiping my runny nose against my shoulder. "I'm not telling you that so you'll throw your panties at your date. I tell you that because life goes on despite our jobs. It's too short not to have fun while we can. Sitting at home with guns and silver expecting the worst is no way to live. Trust me on that. I know."

The sweatshirt worked its way down my front, and I shifted to wrap an arm across my chest so my boobs didn't join the conversation. Moving strained my cut some, but not enough to rip me open. Whatever Mom did back there helped. "Listen to you, being all Mom-like and crap."

She flinched. "Cut me some slack, will you?"

"What? You aren't offended by that. Come on."

She shrugged, though it wasn't an easy, fluid thing like she didn't care. It was more like she cared too much and didn't want to show it. "I know I'm a fuck-up. I wasn't raised normal, and I sure in Hell didn't know how to raise a kid, so I had to wing it. It's not a lot, but I'm trying over here."

"It's enough, Mom. Seriously." She stood, escaping the bathroom with a stack of bloody towels. "Mom, it's enough," I called after her, feeling like a jackass. Sometimes, I wished I did that thing where I thought *before* I spoke. Unfortunately for me and everyone else, I had a perpetual case of diarrhea of the mouth.

"Wait." I left my toilet perch to follow her, catching her as she was about to descend into the pit of our basement to do laundry. "Please wait?"

"What?"

"... I'll go on the date."

She forced a smile, taking the basement steps two at a time to get away from me.

HAVE I MENTIONED that I'm a dink? Because if not, let me say it here: I'm a dink. Some girls get the butterflies-in-stomach thing over important stuff like their prom or their first boyfriend. I got them over seeing a guy I'd already pseudo-banged, and screw the stomach butterflies, these were stomach pterodactyls. This felt like an execution, not a dinner date.

I picked a black shirt in case my cut split open—visibly bleeding to death would slash my appeal factor in half—a pair of jeans, and a pair of sandals I borrowed from my mom. The best part was when Mom insisted on painting my toenails the same color as the turquoise beads along the sides of the sandals. I couldn't bend, so she did it for me. They looked cute in a dorky way, and her offer to give me a pedicure meant that the tension from earlier was officially off the map.

"You look great," Mom said from the couch, her bare feet propped on the coffee table. She had a bowl of popcorn perched on her lap. I watched as she threw a fistful at her face, catching more kernels than not, though a few fluffy pieces peppered her pink hair.

"Thanks."

"Do I get to meet him? Or are you hiding me away like your dirty secret?"

I checked my face in the hallway mirror, ensuring my makeup hadn't smeared to make me look like a KISS groupie reject. "If he comes in you can, but he seems shy. I'm not dragging him out of his car if he beeps."

"I'd pay twenty bucks to see you dragging your date into the house by his hair. It'd be reverse Tarzan and Jane."

"Whatever." I grabbed my purse right as a silver BMW pulled in my driveway. I didn't know if Ian was super spoiled or if his parents just liked nice cars, but I had to admit I was impressed—them be nice wheels. "Whoa."

"What?" Mom came to stand beside me, staring at my flashy chariot with envy all over her face. "That's an M3. You can kill him and take his car if you want. I'll help you hide the body. Soylent Green for everyone."

"It's probably his mom's."

"If so, I want to shake that woman's hand. Maybe make out with her." Mom had something of a car fetish, and would stare at glossy magazine photos of Aston Martins and Bugattis like a pervert stared at nudie centerfolds. It went without saying Ian's BMW, borrowed or not, scored him immediate awesome points in her book.

"No killing my date. I might need him later." I hugged her with one arm before heading for the door. "And no making out with his mom. That'd weird him out. Me, too, for that matter."

"Oh, fine. Have fun. Don't do anything I would do," she called after me. "And be careful with that back. It's glued, not stitched."

"Uh huh."

"If he's a bad lay, steal the beemer on basic principle."

"I'm leaving now, Mom."

When I emerged from the house, Ian climbed from the car and smiled, heading towards the passenger door to hold it open for me. He'd forsaken the basketball jersey for an untucked button down shirt, black jeans, and a pair of sneakers so white they had to be new.

"Hey."

"Hey" was still only a three-letter-long greeting, but at least it wasn't "'Sup".

"Nice car," I said, climbing in.

"Thanks. It's my dad's."

"My mom might mug him for it. Just a warning." He smirked and headed around to his side. I reached for my seat belt and winced when my back spasmed. The cut didn't gape or ooze, but it definitely liked to remind me that it was there and sucking whenever I moved.

To Ian's credit, he noticed my discomfort. "You okay?"

"Yeah, went on a hunt and got a war wound last night. It's sore."

"Need a hand with your seat belt?"

I hated admitting it, but I was pretty sure I did. I offered the buckle to him. He was careful not to tug too hard as he clicked it into place. When it neatly bisected my left boob, he went to adjust it, then thought better of it, like I'd mistake his help for groping.

"Thanks," I said, suppressing a smirk.

"No problem. You okay to, like, go out or..."

"Oh, you're stuck with me for the night whether you like it or not."

He glanced at me, the corners of his mouth dropping. His fingers raked through his hair. "I'm not stuck. I wouldn't have asked you to hang if I didn't want to." I wasn't sure if I'd sounded that sarcastic or if he was that sensitive. It could have been a bit of both, which meant this date was screwed from the onset and I'd have been better off staying home and eating popcorn with Mom. Hoarders was on, and they showcased crazy cat ladies.

I am so bad at this.

"Sorry. I didn't mean... crap. We're not out of the driveway and I'm being a bitch," I said.

"Nah. I think we're figuring each other out. We should have done that before, at the party, but—" His face flushed, tiny brushes of color creeping across his cheeks. "—except I was stupid. I'd like to start over if that's cool."

If starting over meant we got past the walking on eggshells bit, I was all for it. The only problem was we'd have to pretend the other night hadn't happened to accomplish it. I needed the other night to happen, or at least, I needed it to happen again. Hopefully he wouldn't clam up on me and get prudish because he thought that's what good guys did for girls they'd wronged. The last thing I needed was to wave my panties above my head like a flag and for him to tell me he respected me too much to consider sleeping with me.

I didn't know how to say those things without admitting the full truth that I was only out for the bang, and I wasn't up for making both him and Julie think I was a psycho hosebeast either. Instead, I said, "Yeah, sure," and forced a smile that would have done a used car salesman proud. He took that as his cue to pull out of the driveway, his arm drizzled over the back of my seat.

"I hope you like Mexican food. Julie picked a place downtown." My treacherous brain immediately skittered back to Mom's horrible fish tacos with their slimy green insides. I must have made an inadvertent 'ugh' noise, because Ian shot me a worried look. "I can call if it's not okay. I think there's a steak place across the street."

"No, no. It's okay as long as no one orders fish tacos. Seriously. Those things are nasty. Like, uber nasty."

"Who eats them?"

I glanced at the dwindling reflection of my house in the BMW's side mirror. "My mom, but she's uhhh... special. So that's no surprise."

"Special? Like snowflake special?"

I laughed before I could stop myself; I wasn't sure if he meant to be funny. The poor guy could be asking an earnest question, yet I assumed he meant, 'Is your mom dumber than pig crap?' If that wasn't the case, all the night's progress was out the window and I'd have to apologize for alienating him with my dearth of social skills. Again. Fortunately, a smug smile played around his mouth. He'd meant it, the jerk. Cute jerk, but jerk all the same. "I'm telling her you said that."

"She's a hunter too?"

"Yeah."

"Don't," he said. "I don't want to die."

"Nah. You're safe. Janice is harmless."

"Is she?"

"Sure."

For the most part.

Sometimes.

Maybe.

WE WENT TO a restaurant on the east side of town. It only seated twenty people and wasn't much in the way of atmosphere, but from the moment they brought out their homemade salsa and tortilla chips, I was in love. The food was amazing, the company was good, and wonder of wonders, Ian had no problem talking when there weren't huge groups of people around.

"How's Liam?" Julie asked right after the main courses arrived. I'd gotten chicken quesadillas, Julie and her date John—the big guy she'd used as a human mattress at the party—got taco salads, and Ian pretended to order fish tacos before getting himself some fajitas. I'd kicked his foot under the table for the fake-out. He grinned.

"Good," Ian said. "His tour's over in four months."

"Sweet." Julie turned to look at me. "That's his brother, my older cousin."

"Ah."

Ian motioned at his chest. "The fifty-eight on my shoulder was his football number. I got it inked when he left for the Middle East. He's got my b-ball number in the same spot."

"Ian's parents are such hippies they took him to get his first tattoo. They're as weird as Janice," Julie said, grinning as she dug into her dinner.

"No one's as weird as Janice."

"Janice is your mom, right?"

I nodded and guzzled my soda, immediately regretting it when I felt the world's biggest burp gurgling up from the depths of my stomach. Somehow I managed to swallow it, but not before I envisioned Uber Belch bursting from my mouth and disgusting everyone in a twenty yard radius. Ian would run out of the restaurant like someone had stabbed him with a fork, and I'd be left alone, thumbing for a ride home.

Not good. From there on out I drank only water.

"Yeah. She hates people calling her Mrs. Anything, and if you do she'll... "

"Wet Willy you," Julie finished with a shudder. "I remember the first time she did it to me. It was so freaking nasty."

"Yeeeeep. Welcome to Life With Janice. We should have our own reality show."

Conversation drifted after that, from Ian and John's basketball schedule to Julie's new job at the grocery store, and inevitably, to hunting. It felt weird to talk about it so openly, especially with strangers, but it was liberating, too. It wasn't a security breach to say what I did aloud. At least, Mom never told me we were supposed to keep it quiet, and all you had to do was look at her gear to know what she did for a living. It was more that talking about monsters made a lot of people uncomfortable, like we aired out society's dirty laundry. Sure, some people wanted to rant about it, mostly about how monsters shouldn't have any rights even if they followed DoPR protocol. Those folks gave us a lot of 'Atta Girls' for putting our necks on the line for the 'good of the world'—which my mom quickly corrected with "you mean fat paychecks"—but most people shied away from the subject. Monsters were scary, and our existence proved that they had every right to be scared. It tended to stifle conversation.

The awesome thing about hanging with people my own age was they didn't have enough sense or cynicism to hide from the topic. It was interesting to them. Sure, they all pictured me like some Blade knock-off, but I dispelled what myths I could, and told them about some of my better cases. I also made sure I included the less-glamorous side of our trade, like ectoplasm spooge baths and bitey pixies. By the time dessert came around, I'd talked so much I'd gone hoarse. I didn't intend to monopolize the conversation; they just asked a lot of questions that didn't have simple yes or no answers.

Julie's fork hit the table and she peeked at her cell phone for the time. "Damn. I was hoping we'd sneak in a movie tonight, but it's way too late. Some of us have school tomorrow. Unlike you, you slacker." She stuck her tongue out at me as she grabbed for her pocketbook.

"Hey, I might have another car key gnome. I hate those bastards. They bite, too. Why does everything bite in my job? It's worse than animal control."

Ian smirked and started to sling his arm over my shoulder, but at the last second he remembered my back and settled for stroking along my bicep. I glanced up at him, he smiled down at me, and before I knew it, we held hands. For a couple seconds, I forgot that I'd only agreed to go out with him out of guilt and desire for The Sex. Somewhere along the line he'd ceased to be a dong-on-legs and graduated to actual person status.

"Time to head home?"

"Sure. It's early yet if you wanna come in and hang out or whatever," I said, feeling my face go hot. "Janice is there, though, so warning."

"Sure. Cool."

Julie noticed my blush, giving me a huge smile. "So cute. We'll see you guys soon. Call me, Maggie. We'll get together next weekend maybe?"

I nodded and walked back to the BMW, wishing I could stuff her 'cute' right up her pert ass. As I climbed into my side of the car, waiting for my date to strap me in like a two-year-old in a car seat, I had one of those epiphanies that took me by surprise. It turned out Janice, for all her flaws and idiosyncrasies, knew what the hell she talked about every once in a while. Life was too short not to go on dates, and this date had been awesome.

CHAPTER EIGHT

IT WAS RIGHT around this point in my life I realized that making plans of any type invited fate to crap all over them. The failed deflowering should have been the first clue, the Plasma visit the second. Inviting Ian back to my house to hang out in my room was absolutely the third.

It wasn't even ten o'clock when his car rolled up my street. He took his time getting there, which was okay with me. It meant we got to talk about all sorts of stuff, like his brother's deployment, what his parents did in Sedona (my initial assessment that they were licking cacti for spiritual growth was not that far off the mark—they'd been holed up in some sweat house for a 'purification ritual'), and what I missed and didn't miss about high school. Everything went well; we were compatible despite having almost nothing in common. Everything was peachy keen leading up to my triumphant return home.

And then it all went to Hell.

The lights were off through the entire house, yet all of Janice's vehicles were in the driveway, so she was home. Mom was a night owl, and the idea of her hitting bed before three in the morning seemed improbable. The shades were drawn—definitely weird—and there was a car I didn't recognize parked at the edge of our lot, the back bumper straddling the line to our neighbor's property. As far as I could tell it was abandoned, no one lurking on the inside, but it was so dark outside, I couldn't be sure there wasn't someone crouched in the backseat.

"Slow down," I said, my voice whisper soft. "Park across the street."

"Everything okay?"

"No. Something's wrong." Ian eased onto the sidewalk. I jerked my seat belt aside, cringing when my back screamed its displeasure. I scrambled out of the BMW, nearly falling on my butt in my haste. The car's door slammed shut behind me, far too loud for comfort, the thunderous clap echoing down the street.

"Do you want me to..."

"No. Stay put."

'Stay put' apparently meant 'vacate his vehicle and follow me into my yard as I jog towards the house.'

"Maggie, wait," he hissed. "What's wrong?"

"The vampire job from yesterday. We nuked some elder's first born. Go back to the car. I don't want you getting killed."

"No! I'm not going to let you go in there alone if it's dangerous."

"Don't have time for this chivalry crap, Ian." I pulled out my keys to unlock the van, sliding the back door open and fumbling for a couple of silver blades that I strapped to my wrists. Mom's crossbow was in the house, which meant I was stuck with the auxiliary stuff. I snagged a few water balloons and a wooden stake, wedging it into the waistband of my jeans.

"But you're hurt."

"I'm fine."

"You can't buckle a seat belt!"

As much as it sucked to admit it, he had a point. But he was cannon fodder, a victim waiting to happen. He might as well be the token slut in a horror movie with a sign that said 'Me First' hanging around his neck. But what else could I do? I could barely move my arms, and the heavy artillery was all inside. I was low on ability, lower on supplies.

I tossed him the water balloons, glad he was quick enough to catch them before they exploded on the gravel driveway. Maybe he wouldn't be as useless as tits on a man after all. "Fine. Stay behind me and have your phone out and ready to dial 911 if it goes bad. No talking in the meanwhile, and if something comes at you, chuck those. They've got holy water in them." I slunk my way toward the house, keeping to the darkest recesses of the yard. Ian followed a few steps behind, surprisingly quiet for a man whose feet doubled as skis.

The side door was unlocked, as I'd left it earlier. I crept through the kitchen, navigating my way around the center island and table. All was still, the only sound my heart slamming in my ears. For all that Janice had her quirks, she was a creature of habit. She might be dancing in her underwear on the kitchen counter, but she did it every night at eleven sharp without fail. Her weird was on a wonderfully predictable time table. Something was definitely up. I had to figure out *what*.

I didn't have to wait long. A loud, angry crash exploded from the living room followed by my mother's shriek and a low groan. My sweaty fingers wrapped around the blades, holding onto them like they were the only reliable things in the universe. I pressed my back against the wall and signaled for Ian to do the same. As much as my gut told me to run into the living room like boobalicious Rambo, I'd been taught better. Patience, move slow, assess the situation—that's how you beat monsters, with your head. They were stronger and faster. The only advantages humans could hope for were common sense, a good plan, and a little bit of luck.

Another thud, a squeal, and my mother let out a scream. I rounded the corner, crouched low, ready to spring. She gasped, and my hand searched for the light switch. Whoever was here had probably killed the electricity, but on the off chance they hadn't, I wanted light. Vamps could see in the dark, like cats. I was familiar with my surroundings and could use that to my advantage, but it paled in comparison to preternatural night vision. I took a deep breath, my tongue slicking over my lips. I could do this if I stayed calm, if I maintained my composure. She taught me everything she knew, it was enough.

Go on three—the lights on three. Countdown.

Three.

Two.

One.

I snapped on the light.

Why did I snap on the light?

Mom was there all right, and she was on the floor, but she was not in the dire straits I'd envisioned. There was no pool of blood, or to-the-death struggle, and I didn't catch a single glimpse of crossbows or guns. Oh no, my dearest mother was straddling some blond guy I'd never seen before, neither of them had on a stitch of clothing, and there were...

Bosoms. Everywhere.

"OH GOD, MOM!"

Awkward did not begin to cover this one.

"Maggie! Oh shit. Oh shit, shit, shit."

"IAN STAY IN THE KITCHEN."

"Ian? That's your date, huh. HI IAN. I'm Maggie's mom. Stay out there... where are your pants, Jeff? Damn it, damn it, damn it. I'm so, so sorry."

I swung around and pressed my forehead to the wall, trying not to stare at the naked people entangled on the floor. Why did this happen? Why? I'd gone on one whole date in my life, and when I got back to my house, my mother was all pale wobbly bits on top of some dude I'd never seen before. Ian probably thought I was a moron to jump to murder before sex. He'd never talk to me again, and worse yet, he'd tell Julie and all his friends how stupid I was.

The desire to insert my head into the garbage disposal was overwhelming.

"Kill me now," I groaned.

"I'm sticking in the kitchen 'til you tell me it's fine," Ian said, his voice lacking the mocking censure I expected and— in my mind—deserved.

"I'm so sorry," I rasped. "I don't know what to say."

"It uhh. It happens." There was a harsh bark of laughter before he added, "My parents exist to embarrass me, so I get it."

"This happens? To everyone? Riiiiiight."

"Well, maybe not everyone, but I mean... you know. It's cool."

I steeled myself and peeked over my shoulder to see if the living room was safe, or if rampant nudity ruled the day. Things were improving; my mother's blond friend hopped around on one leg as he tucked himself back into his pants. Mom had found a long shirt and a pair of underwear, and her fingers combed through the sides of her hair to quell the insanity of 'got screwed on the floor' head.

"You're home earlier than I figured," she said when our eyes met.

"Noooo. Really?"

"Sarcasm's not helping. At all." She wriggled into her pants—which looked suspiciously like a pair of *my* pants— her ears the color of cherries. For once she had the grace to be embarrassed by something she'd done. Good. I wanted to rub as much salt into this wound as possible so she'd never forget the day I choked to death on mortification.

"Right. I'm out of line to want to die right now. Totally." I slipped back into the kitchen and peered up at Ian, doing everything in my power not to shake, scream, or punch holes in the wall near his head. The latter might not convince him I was a well-adjusted young woman who could handle whatever freak-fest fate saw fit to lob my way which, you know, I was. Kinda. "If you wanna go, that's cool."

"Alright."

"Look, I'm sorry. It's..."

"Don't sweat it. Why don't we do something Tuesday night? No game so I could come get you."

I boggled at him, incredulous that after this latest fiasco he'd *still* want to see me. We'd had fun at dinner, but so much fun he could overlook cosmic-scale bizarre after seeing my mom naked? I didn't know about that. He was a guy, not the patron saint of 'putting up with Maggie's bullshit.'

I grabbed his hand and led him back to the side porch. For some reason, I had to come clean about everything *right then and there*, to tell him the whole ugly truth about my intentions at the party. Maybe I wanted to push him away so I didn't have to worry about saving face anymore. Maybe I believed he only talked to me because he felt guilty about nearly boffing me on our first meet-up. But I was as responsible if not more responsible than he was for what went down. He shouldn't have to shoulder me out of some misguided good intentions.

"I need to tell you something before you... I dunno, keep being nice to me."

"Okay?"

"I went to that party with the intent to hook up with someone. Not, like, date them, but hook up. I can't... " I twitched, eye contact so far beyond me it wasn't funny. Instead I focused on the top button of his shirt. "I can't hunt vampires unless I bust my cherry. They smell virgin blood and freak out. I figured I could get a quick lay. I didn't plan on liking you. I do, though, so you deserve to know it wasn't your fault what happened. You don't have to keep asking me out."

"Okay."

And that was it. "Okay". It was the "'Sup" of answers. I frowned, feeling like I'd barf my quesadillas all over him. I dared to glance up anyway, expecting him to be output off by what a skankbag I was, but he smiled. He brushed a finger down my cheek, which inexplicably made me want to cry. I concentrated on the dull throb along my shoulder blade to keep from falling apart.

"I ask you out 'cause you're cool."

"I'm not cool."

"Yeah, you are."

"You barely know me."

He shrugged. "I know enough. And you told me the truth about the party instead which is nice. I'm sorry I didn't... you know." *Finish* hung between us for a moment. "If you wanna go out Tuesday, though, I'm game. I had fun tonight. Even with the weird ending."

I nodded, not sure what else to say. My insecurity niggled at me, saying his motivation for sticking around had merely shifted from guilt to the declared promise of The Sex, but before I could entertain the worry overly long, Ian stooped to brush his lips against mine. It must have been like kissing a corpse—I was as responsive as a rock, and I'm pretty sure I forgot to breathe—but when my brain clicked on that he was being sweet, I was sweet back, putting my hand along the side of his neck and nudging his nose with mine. I hoped he didn't mind the silver flashing near his face. I didn't *actually* poke out his eye with a stabby. It only looked like I would.

"Six on Tuesday?" He asked, a breath away. I looked into his eyes, taking note of the flecks of gray in the blue irises before nodding and promptly bashing my forehead into his. Both of us winced, but then we smiled, and he reached into his pocket for his car keys.

"Never a dull moment, Mags, huh?"

I watched him leave, thinking I shouldn't encourage him to call me Mags. It wasn't the most flattering nickname, what with it sounding like bags, hags, and sags.

From him, I didn't mind it.

"SO, MAGGIE, THIS is my friend Jeff. Jeff, my daughter Maggie."

"Hi."

Mentally, I added *nice to know your name now that I've seen your penis,* but I was pretty sure I should keep the color commentary to myself. I grabbed a pillow from the loveseat and hugged it to my chest, pretending it was someone's head and I could squash it like a zit.

Jeff flashed me a smile, granting me an unadulterated view of his sharp, white teeth. I went too-still, like a deer sensing a predator. Jeff's fangs weren't spiky and wild like the vampire at Plasma, but they weren't human either, more like perfectly interlocking shark teeth. *It couldn't be* I told myself, only it was, and I leaned forward to get a good look, tempted to tear off the lampshade so I could better see the color of his skin.

My mother interrupted me before I got that far.

"Maggie, look. Jeff's last name is... "

"Sampson," Jeff said, offering me a hand. "Jeffrey Sampson." I stared at the outstretched fingers like he offered me pestilence. Jeffrey Sampson was the one star vampire job always on the Monster Finder list. Mom told me tagging jobs paid low and weren't worth the risk, that's why she left him alone. Now I couldn't be sure if that was true or if she didn't want to tell me she humped rotters.

He realized I wouldn't shake after a moment, and his hand vanished. "I came because your mother said you two crossed an elder's first born last night."

"By 'came,' do you mean...?"

"Margaret."

Mom stalked towards the kitchen to grab a beer. She handed it to Jeff, he popped the top off, she took a long haul. There was a familiarity to the interaction that lent me pause; by all appearances, they were more than comfortable with one another, so they'd been playing hide the pickle for a while. Since I never went anywhere because I had, like, no friends, I had to assume they did their sweaty monkey business at his place, when she was off doing jobs. Handjobs and blowjobs were part of the repertoire now, too, apparently.

"Let's get this out of the way." Mom slid in beside Jeff, and he rubbed her leg from knee to thigh and back again. "I know what you must be thinking." Considering I contemplated ways to murder my mother's sex buddy with the weapons attached to my arms, she took my thought process well. "We're friends, we've been friends for a while. Jeff helps me with cases sometimes, points me in the right direction. Over time we..."

"Your mother's an amazing person," Jeff interjected. "I've never met anyone like her."

I stared at him, my cheek ticking. On one hand, I could appreciate that he regaled me with Janice's good qualities. On the other, the fact that it came from the *walking dead* who'd *porked her...* it didn't do a lot to improve the mood.

"I'm glad I met her," he added as an afterthought. "She's good for me."

"Really glad, by all appearances. Super glad. Like, erection glad," I said.

"Stop it," Mom warned.

"No! You stop it!" I threw the pillow at her face. She batted it aside before it struck her nose. "You're the one who told me they're untrustworthy monsters. God, Mom, when I walked in here, he probably smelled that I was a virgin and had to do a gut-check on whether or not he'd eat me."

"You overcome that after the first fifty years or so," Jeff said, trying for helpful but only succeeding in making me want to stake him through the face. Or the crotch. At least if I went for the junk he couldn't stick it in my mom anymore.

I ignored the comment, too busy being pissed to pay him much mind. "What am I supposed to think? 'Head down, stay alert, listen more than talk.' Those are things *you taught me* about dealing with vampires. 'They're hunting you as much as you're hunting them.' Does that one ring a bell?"

She guzzled the rest of her beer. "There are exceptions to every rule. Jeff's an exception."

"Why?"

"Because he's earned my trust. He helps me, I help him, both of us live longer for it. But more than that? Because I say so."

"What a load of crap."

"Goddamn it, Margaret. This is my house, and last I checked I'm the one who gets to make decisions about what's okay and what's not." She leaned forward, her hands braced on her knees. "I'm sorry you brought your date home to that. It's embarrassing for everyone, and I'll apologize to his face the next time I see him."

"'If' you see him, you mean. With my luck he'll bail on me."

"If he does that over seeing a pair of tits you're better off without him." She pinched the bridge of her nose and slumped back into the couch, the cushions WHOOSHING beneath her weight. "I'm sorry. I'm angry and... Jeff and I got talking about the Plasma thing, things happened, it was a bad call. Not what we did, but the timing of it."

"Oh, so boinking a dead guy's cool, just not when someone will find out about it?"

Her eyes jerked up to meet mine. "Not when *you'll* find out about it. I knew you'd react like this, and frankly, I didn't want to deal with it. You're a pain in the ass sometimes."

My jaw set as I looked over at the lamp. "What do you want me to say?"

"Nothing, for once. Shut up and say nothing."

"I can't do that."

Mom sighed. From the corner of my eye, I saw her take Jeff's hand, her calloused, scarred-up fingers intertwining with his too-pale ones. "I know you can't, and I'm not going to lie. It sucks."

CHAPTER NINE

I FLOUNCED TO my room, stomping my feet, slamming my door, and pulling a diva-scale tantrum. I propelled myself onto my unmade bed, face buried in a pile of pillows. I decided I wouldn't think about any of this tonight, I'd go to sleep, it was better to leave dramatically so Mom would know exactly how upset I was—in case I was so subtle she didn't understand it the first time.

The only problem with this plan was I couldn't sleep when riled. I rolled over so much I wore a Maggie-shaped indentation into my mattress. When I heard footsteps downstairs followed by the closing of the front door, I willed my mother to come smooth things over now that corpse-boyfriend was gone. That usually happened when we quarreled, anyway. Neither of us liked to go to bed mad. We always made up before sleep time, regardless of the reason for the squabbling. This time it didn't happen. Even an hour later, she kept to herself, choosing the company of the TV over me.

Desperate to make things right, I decided I'd be the bigger person, I'd make the first peace offering. For a few minutes, I had myself convinced I was some great Samaritan, the reincarnation of Mother Teresa. I tiptoed downstairs, careful not to do anything that might be construed as a declaration of war, like stomping my feet or cussing arbitrarily. I hovered around the sixth step, peering at her in the living room. It was dark save for the TV casting flickering shadows over the wall. I knew she could see me standing there like a dumbass, but she didn't lift her head. She sipped her beer and watched whatever was on late night cable.

"Hi," I said.

No answer.

"Whachya watching?"

Silence.

I shuffled my weight from one foot to the other, clearing my throat as I tried to figure out how to broach the beast. "I saw this lamer soft core porn on Skinemax last night. I don't get why they can show, like, all the boobs in the world but we don't get to see one wang. If I wanna see boobs, I'll look at my own."

I dared to step down a few more stairs and paused on the landing. She'd adopted a strange, mechanical routine since I started talking: lift beer bottle to lips, take a long drink, put bottle back in lap, lift remote control, hit the channel button, drop the remote, grab the bottle again, rinse, repeat. I knew what this meant; making nice-nice was not going to be easy. She was fond enough of the vampire that we'd argue about him.

Awesome.

"Look, we should talk."

"It's not always about you," she snapped, jerking her face up toward me. She was so angry her eyes were rimmed red, and a vein pulsed along her temple. "You're embarrassed by what I did, fine. I apologized. It was stupid. But I'm embarrassed, too. You were a rude little shit to a good friend of mine. Worse? He gave me a list of elders in the area tonight who might be looking for us after the Plasma kill." She lifted up a manila folder, waving it around before letting it drop onto the coffee table. The insides spilled out in a fan of papers and pictures. "He might have saved your ass and you were a bitch."

The Mother Theresa thing flew out the window. If she wanted a fight, we'd have a fight, and I'd win because I could point out the obvious flaws in her logic, like the part where The Sex with vampires was okay. Not that she brought that up right then, but I wasn't ready to let it go yet.

"Oh, come on! I wasn't that bad! And you should have told me about him before so I had time to process. You dumped him on me out of nowhere. I didn't realize necrophilia was your thing."

"SEE? That's *why* I couldn't tell you!" She stomped towards the steps, her fingers wrapping over the stair rail as she leaned forward. I walked backwards until my back pressed against the wall. I'd never seen my mom so mad before, and even though I was mad too, she freaked me out. She wouldn't hurt me or anything, but no one stood next to a bubbling volcano without getting burned, and right then she was Mount Vesuvius on the cusp of blasting a big lava load.

"I couldn't tell you because everything's black and white with you. There's no room for gray. Everyone's an asshole, everything sucks, everything's this way or that, never in between. Well, that's not life, Margaret Jane. Nothing is ever absolutely one way or the other. Jeff's a good guy."

"He's a vampire! He sucks blood to live! From living people! He's a glorified leech, and *he's dead!*"

That was the wrong thing to say. Her eyes did a creepy bulging thing, and there was a sound reminiscent of a cat with its tail stuck in a door. I expected her to scream, but instead she turned around, went back to the TV, and adopted the beer/remote control rotation again. She dismissed my presence like I'd become a ghost. I stood there with my back to the wall, unsure of what to do. I'd done some amazingly stupid stuff in the past, but she'd never gotten this furious with me. A small, lizard part of my brain suggested I should apologize, but if I was too pissed off to think straight, the sorry wouldn't mean much. Besides, someone should know what they're apologizing for before they made amends.

I crawled up to my room, letting Mom do her seething anger thing. Hopefully, she'd be over it tomorrow. I'd have a crappy night's sleep in the meanwhile, but maybe when we were both less wound up, we could talk. As I slid between the sheets, feeling lower than crap, I convinced myself that we'd find some common ground in the morning, this was a minor setback in the scheme of things.

Whoa, was I wrong.

MOM WAS GONE when I dragged my carcass out of bed. I stumbled through the living room, catching sight of the MF list hanging from the edge of her desk. It had today's date on it and a circle around a two star goblin job in Hanson with the words 'I'm here' written in Janice's hen-scratch. Apparently, she was mad enough to leave me behind on jobs I was more than qualified to handle.

"Shitty shit, shit!"

I wadded the list into a ball and threw it at the trash bin, missing by a mile not because of lack of skill, but because I have the motor function of a squirrel with brain damage in the mornings. It didn't help that I was exhausted. My sleep was terrible, partially thanks to my mom problem, but also because I had nightmares about Allie's leprechaun buddy all night. I dreamed he chased me around the house with a fireplace poker. It wasn't conducive to proper rest and relaxation.

On the bright side, at least my shoulder didn't hurt anymore. There was some tightness when I moved a certain way, but my answer to that was to not move that way again, problem solved.

I consoled myself with a bowl of Lucky Charms, saving all of the marshmallow bits for last. My second bowl was not because I was hungry, but because I figured if I ate so much I exploded my mother'd be sorry she left me behind. I was about to dig in, but a knock on the door interrupted my marshmallow heaven. Considering we were visited by precisely no one, I found it strange, but I chalked it up to UPS or the postman. I patted my bedhead into place and made for the door.

Being greeted by a wall of ghoul before ten was not what I expected.

Ghouls were human servants who did their vampire master's dirty work during the day. It wasn't that vampires couldn't go out, more that they shouldn't. Post dawn, their powers were diminished: they were lethargic, got terrible sunburns, and—funny enough—they were as blind as bats in bright light, cliché totally intentional. They functioned better at night, so they kept a stable of humans to run around and do their vampire business for them when the day star burned. In this instance, vampire business entailed two strangers standing shoulder-to-shoulder in my doorway looking weird and intimidating respectively.

To be fair, I didn't immediately know they were ghouls. It's not like they wore signs around their necks or scratched it into their foreheads, though I should have guessed what they were by the way they looked at me. It was an amalgam of pity, intensity, and curiosity, like they had a vested interest in me. Considering I was about as interesting as three-day-old bread, it should have set off alarms.

The guy on the left, the previously mentioned weird one, was tall and thin, with a helmet of black curly hair, dark skin, and a series of strange marks peppering his face and neck. They weren't zits or measles, more like chicken pox that had been scratched until they scarred. He wore big clothes on lean bones, so both shirt and pants looked precariously close to falling off if he moved the wrong way.

The other was a woman with shoulders as wide as a refrigerator. Her hair was bleached shock platinum, a kerchief covering her dark roots. A sweatshirt, jeans torn before they saw a store rack, and a smear of thick makeup completed her look, which was... I honestly don't know. Fashionable hobo? Hooker-chic? Admittedly the only thing trampy about her was the cosmetics: eye shadow as blue as a summer sky, red lips that would have done Bozo proud. It looked out of place on such a big lady; she wasn't fat, just huge. One of her hands could have palmed my face like a basketball. She had to be six and a half feet tall.

"Is Janice home?" She asked with a thick accent my television education suggested was Russian. She didn't bother to smile or look me in the eye, instead using her impressive height to peer into the house over my head. The only way I could have stopped her was to jump up and down like a hyperactive poodle, which I was not about to do. Besides, I was too full of Lucky Charms to bounce anywhere.

"Uh. Who are you?"

"Does not matter. You are Maggie, yes?"

Anyone unwilling to give their name was not someone I wanted or needed to talk to. I started to close the door, intending to double bolt it and find myself something explodey or pointy, but the woman jammed her booted foot in at the last second, her hand gripping the side.

"Let go!"

"I am sorry, but you need to come with us now." She pressed forward, and my feet slid over the hallway tile. Not only was she enormous, she was *strong like bull.*

"Screw you!"

"Please. This is nothing bad, just a meeting. Let us do this easy. We will have you home by supper, I am promising."

"Fuck. Off." I didn't have a lot of time to mull my options. The weapons were all in the breezeway, I was losing ground, and the skinny guy swiped for me with his spindly arms. My brain filtered through six zillion Janice-teachings, trying to pick the right one for the given situation, but none of them resembled 'giantess shoving her way into your house and demanding you go for a joy ride.' The best I could do was 'any encroaching enemy should be sized up, and if you're feeling out-manned, run like Forrest Gump.'

Considering I'd developed a justifiable fear of huge Russian women, I felt pretty confident turning tail and screaming through the house like my underwear were on fire. I heard the strangers coming, her lumbering like an ox, him moving fast. Way too fast, like vampire-from-Plasma fast. His arms locked around my chest and he slammed his knee into the back of my leg, destroying my balance. I tumbled forward, but before I could greet the floor face-on, he rolled with me, positioning his body so he'd take the brunt of impact on his back. He wasn't much of a cushy thing to land on being all thin-skinned and angular, but it was far better than busting my nose on the tiles.

Russian hooker lady collected me from him, looping one arm around my torso, the other around my legs. I kicked, I squirmed, I thrashed—it didn't matter. All the hand-to-hand training in the world did nothing against her strength. If I had the smallest window of opportunity, I could gouge at her eyes or hit a pressure point in her neck, but she had me so effectively locked down, I was pretty sure she'd done this kidnapping thing a time or twelve before.

"What are you, werewolves?" I demanded.

"Nyet. We serve Maxim."

My clever brain jumped to 'men's magazine with boobs on the cover' and 'pads', but I swallowed both musings AND a near hysterical bubble of laughter. "That's the vampire elder, isn't it?"

"A prince."

"Wait, a vampire prince?"

"Da."

I figured out two things then. First, Mom and I hadn't nuked any elder's first born—we'd done a prince's first born, and princes were like territory leaders. They acted as liaisons between their communities and the human communities, and as such had a lot of pull. We were in much deeper crap than we'd anticipated. Second, my kidnappers were ghouls. I didn't know much about the hows and whys of the vampire/ghoul bond thanks to that whole 'while a virgin, no vampire stuff for you' clause, but at least I was familiar with some basics. The bond between a master prince and his human servants was mutually beneficial: the vampire got some lackeys to do his grunt work, the lackeys inherited a few supernatural tricks for their veneration. In this case, it was improved strength and speed, though I'd read about some ghouls with telekinesis, telepathy, and shapeshifting.

I glanced back at the skinny guy. He slithered along behind us, stopping when we hit the threshold to close the front door of the house. He hadn't said a word, letting my Amazonian captor do all the talking, though when I stared at him, he smiled. I would have smiled back except for that whole *being terrified and pissed off and wanting to bite off his face and maim him for life* thing.

We piled into an SUV with tinted windows, me crammed tight to the woman's chest like an overgrown infant. Before I could holler my head off for one of the neighbors to call the police, she shoved my face into the side of her boob, stifling my cries. I dug in my teeth to give her one to remember me by, but her sweatshirt was too thick to get through. Not only was I frustrated, but now my tongue was all linty, too. It sucked.

The door closed shut and the car moved. As the two ghouls were in back with me, a third person chauffeured, but there was a privacy shield between driver and passengers so I couldn't see who it was. It hit me then that I was going to see a vampire prince, that I had been taken from my home and was now considered the victim of a monster attack. The lady said I was safe, that I'd be home by suppertime, but she probably lied and I'd be bitten and bled dry. I never should have been a pain in the ass about the journeyman thing, I should have waited 'til Ian did me right, this was all my fault.

The worst of my woe-be-gone epiphanies? I'd been a dink to my mom the night before my imminent death. I'd be forever immortalized as 'that kid, the dink.'

A high-pitched squeal erupted from my lips, a sound similar to a whistling teakettle, and then I burst into tears. My giant Russian friend bounced me in her lap with quiet tuts, effectively ramming my forehead into her jiggling funbags. Too much more of it and she'd knock me out before we got to where we were going. I wasn't so sure that was a terrible thing.

"Do not cry, malyshka. I am Lubov. This is Ahmed. No tears. It is as I said—a meeting. Nothing more."

Tears became sniffles, sniffles became sobs, and I went slack in her arms, accepting her offered comfort. I hated her, of course, and was angry she'd taken me, but she sounded so earnest that I'd survive, I needed to believe she wasn't all bad. If she was, that meant she was a liar, which in turn meant I'd be dead by nightfall. Well, dead by nightfall *if* I was lucky and they didn't torture me first.

When Lubov the Kidnapper crooned in Russian, reciting a brownie recipe for all I knew, I went boneless and sniveled, lamenting my helplessness like a big, snotty pile of fail-hunter. She stroked my hair and I closed my eyes, wishing I hadn't let my mother down by being stupid enough to get kidnapped.

CHAPTER TEN

AN HOUR LATER, the car rolled to a stop. Lubov had let her iron grip slacken—enough that I had some wiggle room, not enough to execute any grand escapes—but when the driver's door thudded shut, it was back to my face getting planted in her mammaries.

"Put me down," I growled. The sole remnant of earlier's breakdown was the headache pounding behind my eyes. There was some satisfaction in knowing I may have been a big crybaby about things, but at least I'd gotten snoogers on one half of the kidnapping team.

"I will, but if you run, Ahmed will catch you and we will tie you until home time. Do not make this happen." Before relinquishing her hold, she walked me inside a high rise building. I took note of the traffic sounds, the hustle and bustle of people coming and going around me—all of them oddly blind to the teenaged girl drowning to death in Russian sweater puppies—and I recognized Boston. Lubov carried me to the elevator, stepped inside, and Ahmed pushed the button to the appropriate floor. Halfway up, I was deposited back onto my bare feet. Lubov moved in front of the elevator controls so I wouldn't do something spectacularly clever like pull the fire alarm or buzz the front desk and announce that I'd been forcibly removed from my home by a quasi-vampire streetwalker.

The elevator dinged at the forty-fourth floor. As soon as the door opened, I was pushed into an ultra-contemporary apartment suite complete with bubbled glass walls to my left and right, stainless steel overhead lights, and a Japanese-looking fountain drizzling water onto polished, ovular stones. It was industrial meets museum, too chic to feel homey, and I hunched down, feeling ragged and dirty in comparison to my surroundings.

I glared over my shoulder at Lubov, letting her know without words I didn't appreciate having to go first. She was impervious, though, flashing me a smile wrought with crooked, yellow teeth. Bad though they may be, at least they were human looking. That put her above Prince Maxi Pad, or whatever the heck his name was.

Wave and water sounds spilled through the foyer. I eyeballed the fountain, wondering why it had gotten louder. Upon closer listen, I figured out the house was wired for surround sound, and that there were nature sounds playing, like those cheap CDs you could get from the dollar store. This wasn't exactly the dirty warehouse murder scene I'd anticipated; it was far too clean and lacking blood. Where were the salivating vampires hanging from the rafters? Where were the mauled carcasses?

Why was that guy doing Pilates in the front room?

"Maxim, this is Maggie."

Pilates man, or Pilates vampire to be more specific, stopped bending over backwards to peer at me. He wasn't particularly tall, nor was he very old looking, though I knew that meant jack and squat as far as true age went. He had unremarkable brown eyes, less remarkable brown hair, and a lean, fit frame. He also wore a pale gray track suit and had bare feet that—I couldn't help but notice—had seen a recent pedicure. The whites on his toenails were far too bright to be natural.

"It's Max now, Lubov. Maggie, sit. Please."

"... no thanks."

"Please. *Sit.*"

There was an emphasis on the word that wasn't harsh so much as emphatic. Normally, I'd go out of my way to tell him to shove it where the sun don't shine, but before I could mouth off, my feet shuffled towards the couch and my butt planted itself down on a cushy seat. My body had betrayed me; my brain said to do one thing, the rest of me did another at his behest.

"Hey. Hey!"

He smiled, completely unrepentant that he'd made me his human puppet, and sat across from me, using a small white towel to dab at the back of his neck. Ahmed came to stand behind him, putting a hand on his shoulder and squeezing. Maxim's fingers laced with his, and they shared a smile that could have melted butter.

"Ooooh. Oh, I get it." I hoped they didn't take that wrong, like I marveled that they were queer. I didn't care that they were together any more than I cared that Tiny Tina and Allie were together. It was more that Ahmed had gone out of his way to ensure I hadn't been hurt in my kitchen. He'd rolled so he'd take the brunt of fall impact in my stead because his boyfriend told him to. Maybe Lubov's promises that I'd make it out of here alive were true. That'd be nice. I had important things left to do in my life, like sleep with Ian and watch that TLC reality show about pregnant teenagers huffing paint. Or was that teenagers who ate paste dating paint huffers? Whatever.

"We need to discuss the Plasma thing, Miss Maggie. I don't want to make this more upsetting than it already has been, so please know I'm sorry I had you removed from your home. I simply didn't see you or your mother coming along of your own accord. Neither of you are particularly friendly towards my kind, and it's important we talk." He motioned at Lubov. "Get the girl a drink, would you? She's a guest."

"I'm not thirsty."

"Yes, you are."

And then I was thirsty. Neat trick, that.

"Stop dicking around with my head. You can't apologize one minute and play with my mind the next. That's not cool." I looked around the apartment, hoping to spot something wooden that'd make a suitable stake if things went bad. Well, worse. I had a snowball's chance in Hell of topping him, but I wouldn't sit there while he mashed my brain like a pile of Play-Doh. The problem was there didn't seem to be a single suitable thing in the entire suite. It was all metal and glass. Even the kitchen cabinets were stainless steel, blending seamlessly with similarly fashioned appliances.

"I'm not using mind control. This was gleaning the obvious." Maxim motioned at my feet. "For example, you worried about your appearance earlier, when you first came in. I sensed the insecurity. Just now, I sensed your thirst, which I can't blame you for. After all, you only had... " He cocked his head to the side. "Oh, Maggie. Yuck. Lucky Charms are a terrible breakfast."

"Lucky Charms are awesome. Shut up."

That's it, Maggie. Defend your cereal choices 'til your dying breath. Possibly literally. Focus, you boob.

AWESOME

He tittered, and I knew he'd skimmed my surface thoughts. "You're going home as whole as the day you came into this world. Please stop thinking otherwise. And, yes, I have some power of suggestion, but my talents are more in sensing than directing. I'm harmless in comparison to other vampires."

I kinda doubted the harmless thing considering he was a prince, but I wasn't brave enough to tell him he was so full of crap it leaked from his ears. Lubov cracked a can of Coke in front of me and poured it into a funky, multicolored glass that looked like it came from Wonderland. The bottom was clear and see-through like normal, but along the top it was rainbow colors and wavy warps. As the soda snapped and fizzed, I realized how badly I wanted it. I hadn't had any juice earlier, nor had I guzzled the milk from my bowl—Lubov and Ahmed had interrupted a sacred breakfast ritual of 'consume mountains of cereal, relish sugary, diabetic-shock-inducing moo juice.' Max sensed a thirst I hadn't gotten around to acknowledging because I'd been distracted by the whole kidnapping thing.

I guzzled the Coke, telling myself it was okay because Lubov had opened the can right in front of me, it hadn't been tampered with or there'd be no bubbles, and I'd seen the roofie-free bottom of the glass. It tasted fine, like Coke ought to taste anyway. I could remain fairly confident I hadn't poisoned myself with a glass of carbonated Mister Clean.

"So what do you want?" I asked when half the glass was gone.

"Let me say this first: I understand why your mother did what she did. My fledgling was stupid and returned for a second taste, and her handler was stupider still for letting her go. However, I think parking a pure girl such as yourself

113

near Plasma invited trouble." He paused to cast me a sly look, and I saw Ahmed's smile ratchet up a notch. Great. Vampire and vampire's boyfriend both thought a seventeen-year-old virgin was ridiculous, too. I might as well wear a FAILED THE SEX badge on my forehead. "Irregardless, she was wrong to attack you."

He looked like he expected me to say something to that. The best I could muster was, "It's regardless. The I-R is redundant."

Yeah. I showed him.

"You're such an odd creature." His smile told me that wasn't a bad thing. In fact, I'd have almost said Max-the-Pilates-Vampire *liked* me, which was weird to think about. "But, yes, I'm sorry for what happened. Truly. The problem is this whole thing has gone..." He paused, shrugged, and then smirked. "Wonky. I didn't want a progeny to start with. They're high maintenance, but I accepted one as a condition of peace between myself and the prince immediately to my west. Lizzie is—well, was—a living descendent of his line. When he found out that she'd been killed, he demanded to know by whom, and the terms and conditions of our peace agreement were nullified." He watched me sip my Coke for a long moment. "If I may ask, how long has your mother been hunting in Massachusetts?"

"Her whole life."

"And she's what? Thirty-six?"

I nodded.

"So young for such a sordid reputation. The problem is, Miss Maggie, it's been a very industrious thirty-six years. She's killed a lot of my kind—everyone knows someone she's exterminated." He folded his hands together, elbows balanced on his splayed knees. His smile remained bland, but there was something else to it, something *knowing* that put me on edge. I fidgeted in my seat, wondering what I missed, why Mom's job—which had never been a secret in the first place—was a factor here.

"So glad you asked," Maxim said. I tapped my temple and scowled, he ignored me to keep talking. "I'm keeping the details of Lizzie's death quiet while I arrange a new peace agreement. If Matthew discovered the particulars of her demise, it'd cost me and arm and a leg in restitution. In the meanwhile, though, because he's an impatient ass, he's put a bounty on the killer. I sincerely doubt your mother's government status would deter some of his brood, especially the ones who've lost loved ones or friends in the past."

He splayed his hands and peered at me, allowing me to compute. When it sunk in, I felt sick. Prince Matthew had effectively sicced every vampire, werewolf, witch, and spookier-than-thou thing in his domain on my mother. The only thing stopping them from splattering her within the next day or two, and me by extension, was this prince's silence about who was responsible.

I collapsed into the couch. Within the next few days, Mom would file paperwork on the Plasma incident. For all that she had the jurisdiction to nuke monsters when they broke the law, she had to create a paper trail so it didn't look like an arbitrary slaying. There were *some* laws in place to protect the oogedy boogedies. The problem was if she did that, the files went public. She'd be advertising that she was guilty to everyone wanting a piece of Matthew's promised pie. It was like tying a pork chop around her neck and walking into a den of starving wolves.

"Precisely," Max said.

"... she can't... she has to... "

"Yes."

"I need to tell her... damn it." I put down my glass of Coke and stood, no longer compelled to sit, my eyes swinging to the door. I wanted to run home and tell her as soon as possible. We may have argued last night, but there's no way it'd hold up against this. Priorities and all that crap. My hands braced on the back of the couch, fingers squishing into the leather cushion. "I'll tell her to keep it quiet. I'll tell her about it and... "

"It's not so simple. I wish it was, but the fact is if she finds out I removed you from your home, she'll come after me for kidnapping. You know it, so do I. And if she comes in guns blazing, I have to defend myself and my interests." That impassive smile returned despite his veiled threat. He stood, stretching his arms over his head to do some funky-looking yoga maneuver. When he spoke again, I couldn't see his face because he was bent in half. Secretly, I hoped he lost his balance and ended up with his head wedged up his ass.

He stopped looping his leg behind his head long enough to peer at me. "Your job, Miss Maggie, is to stop your mother from filing that paperwork *without* mentioning our visit. Keeping this conversation quiet helps me, helps you, helps her. I don't care what you tell her about Matthew, but leave me out of it. Understand?"

I frowned at him, and by association the challenge before me. How was I supposed to explain everything without mentioning the talking to him part? "Hey Mom, the tooth fairy stopped by and said you're boned if you don't keep your trap shut about that Plasma kill" didn't quite cut the mustard, nor did, "Hey, a little bird told me some territory prince has a bounty on your head!" Mom'd want a better explanation than that. Besides, any time she thought I hid something from her she was like a bloodhound sniffing a trail: unrelenting. It wasn't that she didn't trust me, more that she was that nosy.

"I can't do that."

"Yes, you can. And you will."

Sure, I will, Asshole. Sure I will.

I cringed as soon as I thought it, knowing he probably 'heard' it, but he said nothing so maybe it slipped by. One could hope, anyway.

"Now then, did you have any other questions? Anything I can do for you?"

"Uhh. No, I don't think so."

"Excellent. Lubov will give you my telephone number should you need to contact me. Remember, Maggie, you won't tell a living soul about our arrangement."

"Sure."

I had every intention of bringing him up. I had every intention of telling Mom *everything* and explaining why she shouldn't go after Max despite his heavy handedness. Too bad I forgot that the road to Hell was paved with good intentions.

CHAPTER ELEVEN

KIDNAPPED, BROUGHT TO a vampire prince's den, and back before two in the afternoon. All in all, it was an efficient crime and, for all that I'd piss and moan about it, far less scarring than it could have been. I had all of my limbs, all of my blood, and I hadn't peed myself. For reasons I couldn't understand, Lubov insisted on carrying me into the house. She deposited me on the couch as gently as, say, she'd throw a sack of onions on the floor.

"It was nice to be meeting you. You are good girl."

"Uhh, sure, Lubov. Thanks. Now get out."

She waved like we were old friends before heavy-stepping back to the SUV. I scrambled to the front windows to watch the car pull away. As soon as they were out of sight, I rifled through Mom's desk crap, looking for the slip of paper with her latest phone number on it. I found it stuck to a Post-It note on the back of a pizza menu. I dialed frantically, hoping she'd take the call. After about six rings she picked up, and I heard her turning her Bon Jovi down right as Richie Sambora wailed "WANTED" at the top of his lungs.

"Yeah?"

"Hey. Uhh, sorry to bother you, but earlier today I..."

The rest of the words died, like Max choked them out of me through the phone line. I felt pressure on my throat, invisible fingers squeezing my explanation away. I gasped and rasped, desperate for air. I must have been panting or wheezing aloud, because my mom repeated my name over and over, her tone rising in urgency when I couldn't answer.

"Maggie? Maggie. Margaret!"

"Mom. I..."

"What's going on?"

The more I struggled to tell her I'd been taken from the house, the more lightheaded I felt. Blood rushed to my face, my head swam, and I got so dizzy I nearly dropped the phone. Somehow I kept my grip, though I had to stagger to the couch to sit so I wouldn't puke or pass out in the middle of the floor. My chest constricted and my tongue felt heavy. One time, before I'd been expelled from school, I'd seen a girl get stung by a bee at recess. She was allergic and went into anaphylactic shock. Her face turned blue, she twitched, and her eyes rolled up into her head. That's how I felt, then—like I'd introduced a toxin to my body and every fiber of my being rebelled against its invasion.

"Can't... breathe."

"I'm about twenty minutes from home. Do I need to call an ambulance?"

"No. Be okay. Be okay in a min... yeah."

The second I stopped trying to talk about Max, the strangling sensation ceased. My breath came back, my head cleared. The change was absolute, from total body collapse to 'fine and dandy, thanks for asking'. He'd warned me not to say anything, but I thought it was more a suggestion than whatever the hell this was. It was obviously some magic douchery on his part. Not only did it scare the crap out of me, it made me angry. Angrier than I'd been at being taken from the house in the first place.

This bordered on punch-a-bunny angry.

"Maggie? Talk to me."

"Here. I'm here. Sorry."

I snagged some paper from her desk and something to write with, which ended up being a hot pink colored pencil because pens disappeared into the great void of Janice when no one was looking. I attempted to write what had happened, thinking maybe I could get around the 'no sharing clause' with ingenuity, but my hand cramped, every muscle agonizingly tense as I tried to write Max's name. I dropped the pencil onto the floor with a frustrated shriek.

"Mom, I'm... come home. I'm okay, come home," I managed, working my fingers into a fist. Clench, unclench, over and over until the tingling abated.

"All right. Sit tight. I'm almost home, okay?"

"Yeah."

I flung the phone across the room. It walloped against a chair cushion and skittered onto the floor. It would have been so much more satisfying to whip it against the wall and blast it into twelve trillion pieces, but then I'd have no phone at all, and considering what happened earlier in the day, it wasn't worth the risk.

THE SOLE GOOD thing about the morning's shittery was that Mom's concern for my well-being trumped last night's argument. Our fight lingered like a bad smell, but we back-burnered it to concentrate on the matter at hand, which was me gurgling like a broken toilet while I was on the phone. I watched her pace the kitchen, warding off her nerves by keeping busy. Score for me, she produced two heaping roast beef sandwiches in the process. I wasn't hungry, so I picked off the meat, leaving the cheese, bread, and mustard behind.

"You're fine now. Just like that."

"Yeah. I'm okay."

Before she'd come home, I'd tested the lengths of my vocal freedom. I could get away with "I went out today" but the moment I tried to add in anything resembling a detail ("to Boston", "to the city", "north") I locked down. If I lied and said "to a pony farm" or "to store my dead hooker collection in the trunk of your car", that was acceptable. Writing things down worked the same way. Unless I wanted to get adept with smoke signals, Braille, or Morse code real quick, I was screwed.

This presented a fresh, interesting problem of trying to explain my newly manifested health ailments to a concerned parent.

"You're sure you don't want to go to the hospital," she said for the thirtieth time since walking through the door.

"Totally sure. If it happens again, then yeah, but I think I uhh... I dunno. I'm fine now."

She watched me dismantle the second half of my sandwich and hone in on the roast beef. It was so rare it would moo in protest any time now. I was cool with that; the tender pink middle reaffirmed my status as upper-crust food chain. Screw you cows, I'm a predator.

"Something wrong with your bread?"

"No. Not hungry."

"Uh huh."

She pressed a hand to my head, but I batted her away with a quiet growl. "I'm fine. Seriously. Probably swallowed a bug or something."

"Right. A bug. And I grew a schlong. Call me Charlie."

I decided my best tactic would be to change the subject, and fast. I didn't want to sit around the kitchen all day assuring her I was all right—that sounded about as fun as dousing myself in gasoline—so I had two choices. I could bring things back to Jeffrey and repair last night's rift, or I could engage her about Matthew and that whole 'bounty on your head' thing without giving away any actual details. Option two was way harder than option one and required a lot more thinking. The good news was she was bad about paperwork and wouldn't get to the report for at least a couple days. I had time yet.

One it was.

I didn't like that she bumped uglies with a vampire; I found the whole concept reprehensible. But being perfectly honest with myself, she was a grown woman and this was her choice. If she wanted to let the stiff put his stiffy in her...

Gross. Her decision, but gross.

"How does he get a boner? I mean, he has no blood pressure."

I could have broached the subject more delicately, but Mom didn't seem to care. She stared at me for a minute before quirking a half-smile.

"All the plumbing works. But if you want the juicy details, he's good sized with a slight curve to the..."

"THAT'S AN ICK, MOM!"

"What? TMI?"

I threw a piece of mustard-bread at her. She snagged it to take a bite from the crust.

"Nudity's a beautiful, natural thing. Be proud of your body, Margaret Jane. You only get one this life. No point in getting all hung up about it."

"You don't have to share it with everyone!"

"I don't! Just you, Jeff, and your boyfriend. Oops on the last. Sorry."

"One date doesn't make him my boyfriend," I said.

"Touching his winky does!"

"Gross."

We bantered like everything was peachy-keen, but it was stiffer than usual. I rolled my eyes at the appropriate times, and laughed when she joked, but I kept waiting for the other shoe to drop. It was clear she did the same; there were thin lines at the corners of her mouth that belied her good-natured chatter. Things weren't going to get copacetic until we stopped dorking around and approached this thing head on. Which meant, as much as I hated to admit it, eating crow.

"About last night." I skimmed my hand over the back of my neck, my fingers toying with the ends of my hair. "I didn't mean to be rude. I was surprised, and freaked out, and I acted like a douche. I'm sorry."

Her brows shot straight to her hairline. I wasn't exactly known for my grace when I felt I'd been wronged. Actually, I was kind of a stubborn pain in the ass about stuff like this, so I fully expected her to relish the moment, maybe get smug that I owned up to a failure. I couldn't have been more wrong. Her countenance softened, and she squeezed my forearm. "It takes balls to admit when we're wrong, so thank you. And you know what? I screwed up, too. I handled that like all kinds of shit. So let's call a truce, yeah?"

"Truce. I don't like it," I admitted before I could think to shut myself up. "You taught me how bad vampires can be. It's hard to believe everything's gonna be cool. I don't want you mauled or whatever."

"I know. I ask that you give him a shot. And don't be a shit when he's around. I said too much good stuff about you and you'll make me look bad."

"Okay."

She ruffled my hair and then she took off to hit the shower. I gave the MF list a glance to see if there was anything worthwhile to do that afternoon. Outside of the goblin job, there was a minor haunting in Bridgewater and a disturbed grave in Plymouth. I liked disturbed grave jobs; they were always something awesome, like a witch dug up a body for nefarious purposes, a necromancer raised a corpse as a slave, or a voodoo curse had robbed some poor bastard of restful death. Most times we didn't find what happened to the rotter—whoever raised them usually had a purpose in mind, and it wasn't to hang around the cemetery for a great big party—but the hunt was always interesting, and success stories paid well. Plus they didn't pop up all that often, so seeing one on MF was like a deranged treat.

I made my way towards the bathroom so I could holler through the door. "Hey, Mom? Undead thinger in Plymouth. You going?"

"Nope, *we* are. Gear it up. We're outta here in a half hour."

THE LOVE FEST in the kitchen was far less indicative that things were back to normal than the going-on-a-job-together thing. We didn't say much on the drive, but that was mostly thanks to Bon Jovi's Greatest Hits and rolled-down windows. It was gorgeous out, a balmy seventy degrees, and it seemed a sin to coop ourselves up when we could take advantage of sunlight and fresh air.

The cemetery was on top of a hill, near a stone church at least a few hundred years old. There were hotels and restaurants all around—shops, too—which meant we were dead-center of the tourist district. The man who'd called us was with the sheriff's department, and he waited for us near an above-ground sarcophagus. That wasn't where the disturbance was, though. It was two rows back, in front of a new headstone. I glanced at the name carved into the granite, then the date below. Lauren Miller, our missing corpse, buried only two weeks ago. She was twenty-four years old.

The man offered a hand as we neared. He was about 5'4" tall and equally as wide, with a gray mustache and beard, and an embroidered ball cap shielding his eyes and face. "Janice?"

"Officer Tate. Nice to meet you. This is my daughter, Maggie. She's my apprentice and will be assisting me today."

The officer's eyes flicked over me, from my crappy, long sleeved tee shirt to a pair of jeans so ragged the bottoms frayed. I'd trimmed some of the strings before we left the house for fear of tripping if we had to run. "Aren't you young to be doing this sort of thing?"

"Nah. I was too young when I was thirteen, though!"

I gave him an ear to ear grin, and my mother shot me a glare. My hand moved up to cover my boob before she could whack it with her elbow.

"Our trade allows for kids to get in on apprenticeships early, Officer. Like farming or something you'd learn in vocational school. There are restrictions in place for her safety, I promise," Janice said, using that tone of voice she reserved for professional stuff and when people died. It was all sugary and nice and made me want to fake-gag, but I figured she'd pinch me if I acted up so I behaved myself.

Officer Tate forced a smile before motioning at the grave, bringing us back to the matter at hand. "Well, that's all we have to give you. The empty grave. We contacted her family but they don't know a thing and the house checked clear. They're out of their tree upset. The poor kid died of cancer and now she doesn't get a proper death."

"I understand. No sightings?" Mom knelt beside the recess, looking down at the crumbled earth and splintered casket. The coffin was broken from the inside out, not the other way around, which would account for us being called.

"Sightings of what?"

"Undead. The walking dead."

The cop stared at her, incredulous that she'd suggest such a thing. I wanted to point out he'd contacted professional hunters, that he shouldn't be surprised we'd suggest paranormal creatures. Fluffy kittens did not, in fact, mysteriously punch out coffins. "No. You think someone would resurrect a girl like that? Who'd do that?"

"You'd be amazed." Mom smiled at the cop, who swept his fingers down the sides of his mouth and grumbled his distaste. Such blatant discomfort was a sign it was time for him to go. Nine times out of ten non-hunter types screwed up a work site, screaming at the wrong time or becoming fodder because they were too stupid to get out of the way. The ensuing splatter was annoying and hard to work around, so Mom almost always sent them off. The officer was no different. He might have a gun, and he might be trained for rudimentary monster issues, but if the concept of someone resurrecting the dead for evil deeds or some weird corpse-humping fetish made him twinge, he wasn't someone we needed nearby.

"Thank you for calling us, Officer Tate. We'll contact you with our findings. For now, though, it'd be best if we have the area to ourselves."

He didn't seem all that put off by her dismissal. Actually, he looked relieved.

"Sure thing. You have my number?"

"I do."

He meandered off down the hill as Mom investigated the grave for evidence of ritual goods. Voodoo practitioners usually left animal bones or feathers behind. Witches used runes, certain types of candles, and herbs. Necromancers used blood—lots of blood. The funny thing was, she couldn't find a damned thing. Either someone knew we'd be called and were meticulous with their clean-up, or something different and new and freaky-bizarre had gone down. I secretly hoped for the last because... well, because I was weird and found this crap fascinating.

"Maggie, look in the grave dirt? There's nothing by the stone."

I crouched beside the hole, then decided I'd be better getting into it. I was about to plunge in when a strange stink caught my attention, making me cover my face with the back of my arm. It was nasty. Sweet yet sour and chemically, too, I couldn't help but associate it with the formaldehyde used in biology class. Well, formaldehyde and rotting meat.

"Ugh. That's rude!"

"What is?"

"I think I smell her. The dead chick. It's all gross down here."

Mom blinked at me before coming over to hover at my side, stooping at the waist to get a waft. Her forehead crinkled as she leaned further in—so far I thought she'd fall in the hole face first. I steadied her with my hand on her knee.

"Nasty, huh?" I asked.

Her lips flattened into a grimace.

"I can't smell a damned thing."

CHAPTER TWELVE

CONSIDERING ITS PUNGENCY, Mom's obliviousness confused me. I trailed it, stooped at the waist, my face only a couple feet off the ground. Every few feet, I caught another waft of corpse, and I zigged and zagged down the hill, until I stood along the street's edge, traffic buzzing by.

"I think she's that way," I said, pointing at the waterfront.

"Did you sniff out..."

"Shut up, Mom."

She was good enough to close her trap as we jogged across the street and down towards a small park with a bridge and a flock of ducks. The scent got stronger, leading me to a stone bridge with a hidden alcove. There, surrounded by a dozen headless duck and pigeon corpses, was our missing rotter.

Normally, the undead were slathering, brainless messes— pretty much carbon copies of anything you'd see in a Romero movie. This one seemed rather aware for the newly risen. She chewed on a pigeon head, which was pretty off-putting on its own, but as soon as she saw us, she paused, wiping her lips across the back of her arm. She wore her funereal garb: a pale pink dress, a string of pearls, and ballet shoes. Her hair was dark and pulled back into a bun, her skin pale. Besides some sunken eyes and too-prominent cheekbones, she looked pretty good.

Well, for a corpse anyway.

"Hi. Sorry, had to stop for a snack. I'm starving. So hungry. And pigeons seemed easy."

It talked. It wasn't supposed to talk. That was a level of brain function that shouldn't happen. Mom's hand went inside of her vest, likely for her gun, but she was stalled by the girl standing and wiping the feathers from her dress. It was such a human, non-aggressive gesture. We hunted monsters, yeah, but only the bad ones. Friendly, agreeable ones were tagged and re-released into society according to DoPR law. Except I didn't think there'd ever been a friendly, agreeable zombie before, so the protocol was hazy.

Okay, not hazy. Nonexistent.

"They're messy. Pigeons. There has to be a better way to do this." She chewed her bottom lip before looking at us. "I'm Lauren, by the way. I think I died last week but they had me on so many pain medications, I can't remember much. I was sick, though."

"You are," Mom said. "Were. Lauren Miller, I mean."

"I *know* that. I'm dead, not stupid. Who are you?"

Mom dropped her hand and cast me a look that said, "I have no idea what the crap to do with this one." I probably mirrored the expression. This was off-the-charts.

"I'm Janice. This is Maggie."

"Hi. Nice to meet you. Do you have a car? I need a ride home. God, I'm starving." One moment Lauren-The-Zombie stood there smiling at us, the next she was a swooping Valkyrie of duck death, grabbing an unsuspecting fowl from the water and biting into its neck. A squawk, a squirt of blood onto her dress, and it was over. The local wildlife had succumbed to a snack attack.

"Okay, that's messed up," I said, watching her chow down on duck head as casually as a normal person would eat popcorn. "Don't you want, like, a hotdog?"

"Mmm. No. Too processed. I want it fresh. It's gross, isn't it?" Lauren said between bites. She sounded dazed, like reality hadn't hit her yet. I supposed that accounted for her calm. If I woke up zombified, I'd be ripping out my hair and drowning puppies.

"I want the head cheese, too," she continued. "Like, brains and stuff. You smell delicious, by the way, but eating people's wrong so... " She waved the limp duck at us before chucking the carcass into the water. "I'll make do."

I gagged and glanced over at my shell-shocked mother. She opened her mouth like she'd talk, but then she shook her head. "Sure. I mean, I can get you home, but I'm not sure how your family will... I don't think I can take you home 'til we know if you're..." She dropped the thought and sighed. "Do you remember how you were raised? Necromancy's illegal. If you're a victim, we need to find the asshole who did this. Erm. Practitioner. Sorry."

"Language, *Mom*," I said, echoing the tone she used with me whenever I cussed at a job site. She biffed me upside the head.

Worth it.

"I don't think anyone raised me. I woke up. I was alone when I crawled out, anyway. And getting out of the casket was terrible. Good thing I'm strong right now or I'd be stuck down there for who knows how long." Lauren shuddered. "It was a nightmare, climbing out."

"Strong? How strong?"

Lauren walked over to one of the park benches nailed down in concrete, gripped the iron frame, and yanked.

There was the awful squeal of bending metal, a flourish of cement spray, and she held aloft a bench that she'd plucked from the ground like a buttercup. "Like, that's pretty easy."

Mom and I said "shit" in unison.

"So why can't I go home again?" Lauren tossed the bench aside. It landed in the pond with a splash, startling the birds brave enough to linger near the Ted Bundy of duckdom.

Mom pulled out her cellphone. "Because people aren't supposed to raise themselves. You're a potential danger 'til we know how you got out. We don't know if you'll regress and eat people. And I can't put you in a halfway house. There aren't any for your kind. Good Christ. Let me..."

Mom wandered off, her thumb tripping over numbers on her cellphone keypad. I assumed she called the DoPR for instruction. The werewolf, fae, and vampire communities were good enough to fund halfway houses for their brood. The shelters offered job training, instruction on how to operate in society, food, and beds. If Mom deemed a monster a non-hazard, he or she was brought to see a counselor. Because every other type of undead thing was either a mindless slave to a magic type or attempting to stuff kindergarteners into its maw, this lonely smart zombie was screwed. There wasn't a place for her.

I eyeballed her, and she shuffled her feet. I supposed she could turn into a frothing flesh-eater any moment now, but she looked so damned uncomfortable standing there. She kept smoothing her dress and tutting at the dollops of blood all over. Every few minutes, she'd cast guilty glances at the pile of dead birds behind her.

"... maybe she should kill me again," she said quietly. "I'm a freak."

"Uhhh." I had no idea what to say to that, so I bumbled for words and hoped they sounded smart. "Well, do you want to? I mean die. Again."

"Not particularly, but maybe it's for the best? My family doesn't... well, maybe they do. I miss my mom."

I felt sorry for her, though I wouldn't say so aloud. Pity was a funny thing—welcome or not depended on the recipient, and I wouldn't hedge my bets. Still, it had to suck for her. Lauren Miller knew her fate hinged on a phone conversation happening not fifteen feet away in hushed whispers, and she could do nothing about it. She was a walking dead girl who might be exterminated for no other reason than the government said so. But instead of running away in fear or picking me up and stretching me apart like a piece of human taffy, she waited, lost, confused, and willing to accept whatever sentence my mom passed.

Those were not the makings of a societal threat.

Apparently, the government agreed, because Mom flipped closed the phone and motioned us over with a wave. She looked stressed and annoyed. Worried, too, if the fingers twisting the ends of her pink hair were any indication.

"Lauren, the DoPR is opening a case on you and will send a specialist on Wednesday, but for now you're coming with me to my safe room."

"What safe room?" I asked, completely aware that no such room existed. We'd talked about installing one in the backyard a few years back, but having a huge steel box for monster containment was a zoning nightmare in residential neighborhoods.

"The spare room in the basement." Mom offered Lauren a manufactured smile. "We'll clean you up and get you some clothes 'til we have a better plan. I'll contact your mother when we get to the house, okay?"

"Wait," I said, incredulous we'd collected our own stray zombie. "We're taking her home? For serious?"

"Yep."

"But..."

"Later, Maggie."

It was a tone that told me to can it without actually saying to can it. I understood—Mom was on the DoPR's payroll, so if they said we housed a dead girl for a few days, that's what we'd do—but it was pretty screwed up. What if her brain rotted out and she went insane and mauled us in our sleep? What if she was a great actress and wanted to get us somewhere private before she snapped off our arms and sucked the marrow from our bones?

"Crap. What are we going to feed her?"

"I like meat," Lauren offered.

"No shit. Really?" I frowned at Lauren, and Mom jabbed me in the side.

"I'll stop by the store on the way home."

I eyed Lauren. "You're not going to eat the neighborhood pets, are you?"

"Margaret!"

WALMART YIELDED TWO full carts of ground beef and some tee shirts and jeans. Lauren kept apologizing for imposing, and my mom kept saying not to worry about it. *I* worried about it, though. Lauren was a monster, and monsters were for hunting, not inviting into the house. I understood she was different than others we'd encountered but she was still a zombie who'd openly admitted to *wanting* to eat people.

That made her dangerous and scary. Home was a sanctuary, a safe place.

Well, kidnapping stuff aside it was safe.

I didn't know how to voice my concerns without sounding like an unsympathetic turd, but at least there was some consolation in knowing Mom wasn't sure what to make of things either. The main clue? No music playing in the van. It was rare Janice forsook her tunes, but this ride was silent. When we pulled into the driveway, she stuffed four pieces of cigarette gum into her mouth, a weird lump forming in her cheek. She looked like a baseball guy about to spit a wad of tobacco.

"Did you want to give me your Mom's phone number, Lauren?" Mom asked, opening the back door of the van and reaching for some bags. "I'll call your family when we get inside."

"Sure. Thank you."

Lauren grabbed the rest of the Walmart stuff, leaving me with myself to worry about. I'd have called her a show off for being able to carry eighty bags at once with her super strength, but that would imply I wanted to help, and I was perfectly content being lazy.

"All right. After you drop off those in the kitchen, Maggie will show you to the shower."

I almost said "I will?" but I figured that'd land me in the crap again, so I kept quiet and headed into the house. I showed Lauren where to put the bags and then ushered her to the downstairs bathroom, offering her a towel.

"Thanks, Maggie," she said.

I closed the door behind her. A few minutes later, I heard the spray of water. I threw myself onto the couch and turned the TV on, willing my brain to shut down. Maybe I could catch a marathon of *Honey Boo Boo* reruns, or some *Survivor*. Both were known to drop the IQ of the watcher by at least fifty points, and considering the day, I could use some dumbing down. Sadly, Mom wasn't keen on my plan; she emerged from the kitchen with her cell in hand, giving me a heavy look from beneath her brows.

"You're worrying me," she said.

"Huh? Why?" I pushed myself upright on the couch. "I'm fine."

"This morning's gurgling on the phone, then the graveyard sniffing. Is there anything you want to tell me?"

Plenty of things, but I can't. I'd love to, but I can't.

"No, I'm fine. It's been a long day. You know, a zombie in the house. It's freaky. Plus she's... uhh. Stinky." I lowered my voice on the last to not be heard.

"It'll be fine. I'll be careful and... see, that's the thing that's got me worried, Maggie. I can't smell her."

That gave me pause. Lauren reeked, so how was it I had to suppress gags around her and Mom didn't?

"Oh."

"Bit strange, don't you think?"

"I guess?" I shrugged and squirmed back into the couch. "It's the first time I've smelled a zombie, so maybe I'm sensitive to it."

"Maybe."

I could tell by her expression she wasn't convinced. For that matter, neither was I.

I KNEW IAN had basketball practice on Monday night, but that didn't stop me from sneaking into my room to call him at half past eight. Mom was busy dealing with Lauren stuff; Lauren's family was thrilled she was found but not-so-thrilled Mom didn't plant her back into the ground "where she belonged." Lauren took the rejection poorly, and Mom was doing her best to console a weepy zombie, offering platefuls of hamburger meat and handfuls of Kleenex. At least Lauren smelled slightly less disgusting when she emerged from the shower. I could be in the same room without wanting to vomit now.

I could have called Julie to angst over my strange house guest (mostly because I couldn't angst over my vampire kidnapping), but as lame as it was to admit, I wanted to hear Ian's voice. I didn't expect to talk to him, figuring on getting his voice mail, but three rings in I had the guy himself. My guts clenched in the good way, not the 'I have to poop and I can't' way.

"Hello?"

"Hey. It's Maggie."

"Hey. Hi." He sounded happy to hear me.

A smile spread across my face. "Hey. Sorry to bother you. I thought you'd be at practice. Figured I'd leave a message."

"I got out a half hour ago," he said. "I didn't recognize your number so I almost didn't pick up. Glad I did. I meant to ask, like, what you like to do? Making plans for tomorrow night."

"Uhhhh." Self-conscious, stupid Maggie brain rifled through a list of things girls *should* say so I wouldn't look abnormal. Girls liked shopping, right? They liked shopping, and shoes. Lots and lots of shoes. He'd think I was broken if I told him I only owned three pairs, one of which was flip-flops so I wasn't sure they counted. The other two were sneakers and combat boots...

"Mags? You there?"

"Oh. Sorry. Hi. Anything's fine."

He snorted, and I could picture his half-lip curl grin in my head. Thinking about it made me relax. "You sure? You took an awful long time to answer."

"I don't like shoes."

The moment it escaped my lips, I collapsed onto my bed, feeling like a total tool. I wanted to roll over and bury my head under the pillows. That must have seemed so out there to him, like I'd pulled it straight out of my butt.

Ian, for his part, laughed. "'Kay. So no shoes."

"Sorry." Attempting to fit in wasn't working. In fact, I was pretty sure it made me look like *more* of a loser than I was. I decided to try the truth; he said he thought me being a hunter was cool. Maybe, just maybe, he'd decide the rest of me wasn't so bad either.

I mean, I couldn't be the only one who understood how awesome I was.

"I like shooting. Like, at shooting ranges. And I like ghost hunting, especially in cemeteries at night. Video games—fighters, but I'm cool with first person shooters. Uhhh." I took a long, strangled breath. "Anything's fine. We could hang out here or your place or whatever."

For The Sex, I silently added. *I'd be totally fine with The Sex.*

"Maybe after, sure. Have you ever paintballed before?"

"No."

"Nice. Some of my basketball buddies go. I'll give 'em a call. I think you'll like it. Maybe I'll call Jules and John, too. You got some shitty clothes? It's messy."

"Do I have shitty clothes? Hell yes, I do. The shittiest clothes you could imagine. Empress Shitty Clothes the First, reporting for duty."

Ian laughed. "Cool, cool. Six tomorrow night then?"

"Sounds great." And it did. Firing gun-like things at living targets was right up my alley. Better than a semi-formal or a prom, anyway—froofy dresses and updos were terrifying. Semi-automatics? Piece of cake.

"See you then Mags."

Mags. I officially had a nickname. How friggin' cute was that?

CHAPTER THIRTEEN

I DIDN'T EAT or sleep all of Monday night. The food thing wasn't *such* a big deal; I could chalk it up to Lauren's rancid smell. Every time I thought about putting something in my mouth, I caught a waft of grave rot, and my appetite went limper than an old man's wing-wang. The no sleep thing was unsettling, though. I climbed into bed around midnight, willing away my craptastic day, but after an hour of tossing and turning, I gave up. I figured it was nerves about the zombie in the basement, or maybe some residual kidnapping psychosis. Whatever the case, I wandered downstairs to hang out with Mom until I was tired. She had a black and white movie on the television and a beer in her hand. An abandoned bag of microwave popcorn lay by her feet. I pulled up couch space beside her, my feet swinging over to rest in her lap.

"What are you doing back up?" She asked, pressing the cold beer bottle against the arch of my foot. I walloped her with a throw pillow before tucking my legs beneath me.

"I couldn't sleep."

"Why not?"

"Don't know." I craned my neck towards the kitchen to see if Lauren was in there chowing down on hamburger. The lights were off and nothing smelled dead, so I assumed she'd gone to bed. "Is she downstairs?"

"Yeah. Speaking of which, tomorrow I need you to zombie-sit while I'm at headquarters. I'm pretty sure she's not going to maul a neighbor, but I'd feel better knowing you could put one in her brain in case I'm wrong."

I frowned, giving Mom the hairy eyeball from my side of the couch. Sitting around with Lauren all day wasn't a fun prospect. She was way too human to eat soccer moms, so I'd essentially be stuck at home carrying a loaded gun for the sole purpose of watching The View. That felt like a waste of a perfectly good Tuesday, and there were much more exciting things to do, like hunt ghosts and punch pookahs. Maybe stab an elf in the neck for shits and giggles.

"Ugh. Fine. I have a date tomorrow night, though, so as long as you're home by then."

Mom emptied the contents of her beer bottle and let out an earth-shaking burp. "A date, huh? Gonna get down?"

"No. We're paintballing. And *Excuse You*. You're gross."

She grinned. "I'm rubber, you're glue."

"Shut up, Mom."

"Whaaaat?" She winked and settled into the corner of the couch, patting her knee in invitation. I stretched out along the opposite side, my feet returning to her lap. We fell into amicable silence, with Katherine Hepburn waltzing across the flat screen. I had no idea what went on with the story, but everyone looked pretty saying their lines. When the credits rolled forty-five minutes later, Mom wriggled her way out from under me to collect her dirty dishes. She stifled a yawn against her shoulder, her eyes drifting to the clock on the cable box.

"I must be getting old. I'm beat," she said, heading towards the kitchen. "You want anything?"

"No thanks."

She paused to look at me over her shoulder. "What have you eaten today?"

"Half a box of Lucky Charms this morning, and the roast beef this afternoon."

"And?"

"And what? That's it. I'm not hungry."

I thought she'd say something else, maybe argue with me about my inferior nutritional decisions, but she shook her head and disappeared into the kitchen. She emerged a couple minutes later with a ham and cheese sandwich, promptly depositing it onto the coffee table before me.

"Make your old lady happy and eat that. I'm crashing. If I don't see you tomorrow morning, I'll give you a call when I'm coming home from headquarters." She brushed a kiss against the top of my head and headed for the stairs. "Night, brat."

"Night."

As soon as her bedroom door closed, I dissected the sandwich, pulling away the bread and cheese to eat the ham. I wasn't hungry, but pig was too delicious to pass up, so I picked at it while I channel surfed. I figured sooner or later I'd get tired of TV and head off to bed. I figured wrong. When Mom resurfaced at nine the next morning all geared up and ready for the day, I was in the same position she'd left me in the night before. The only difference between then and now was the ham and cheese looked more like a lab experiment than a sandwich thanks to my dissection. Oh, and I was better versed in infomercials.

"Did you sleep?"

"A little," I lied, not wanting to freak her out. I had no idea why I wasn't tired, but I didn't think it was such a big deal. I felt fine. More than fine. I felt spry. Well, the lazier side of spry—I did couch surf for eight straight hours.

"Do more than a little. I can't stand around and argue..." She checked the clock and sighed. "Don't be a shit, Maggie. You need sleep. I'm bringing some burger down to Lauren. If you can check on her later to make sure she's not dying or... uhh..." Mom paused. "You get the point."

"Uh huh."

"I might have Jeff over tonight, but I promise we'll be wearing pants this time."

"Gee, thanks."

She tossed me a wink. "Later, hon. And for Christ's sake, eat something."

She hit the fridge, hit the basement steps, and then hit the road. I stayed on the couch for the next three hours, learning valuable life lessons from TV like Justin Bieber's shoe size and how to get ink out of silk. Lauren never emerged from the basement, and when I went downstairs to check on her she languished in bed, stinking up our sheets. The plate of hamburger meat beside her was empty, though, so I assumed she was still alive.

Well, alive-ish.

"Hey, are you hungry?" I asked.

"No, thank you."

She sniffled and stared at the wall, keeping her back to me. She was all kinds of miserable about her family wanting her re-deaded, and I didn't have the faintest clue how to make it better. It wasn't that I didn't care, I was bad with this stuff. Whenever I felt bad Mom made me laugh. That's how I'd learned to cope with things—cracking jokes—but not knowing Lauren all that well, I didn't want to risk her thinking I was laughing at her expense. I mean, if I said something witty about butterfly bungholes she might take it wrong, and the next thing you know she'd be using my femur as a lollipop.

"If you need something, yell or come on up or whatever," I said. "I'm around to hang."

"Thanks, but I'm all set. I'd prefer to be alone."

"Oh. Okay."

I returned upstairs feeling like a craptastic human being. Lauren needed something, maybe a shoulder to cry on or a duck to maim, and I was too socially inept to provide either, shortage of live ducks notwithstanding. I failed at basic human interaction. Was this a hugging moment? Was I supposed to pat Lauren on the shoulder and say, "Here, here. Mom won't blow your brains out *today*. Tomorrow, though, who knows?"

There wasn't much I could do about it outside of going back downstairs and forcing her to talk. As the prospect made me writhe, I decided I'd take another stab at sleeping. It was escapist and lame, yeah, but also convenient. The problem was I wasn't tired despite being awake for twenty-eight hours. I slid between my sheets and turned on the radio for background noise, willing Calgon to take me away. It didn't happen. I was way too aware. I ended up taking an hour-long bubble bath instead. From there it was a series of mindless activities to fill the hours: video games, throwing a knife at a homemade target, surfing the internet, studying for my GED. Lauren never made a peep. I checked on her a couple more times to make sure she was still there. She insisted she wanted to be alone. Who was I to argue?

The whole zombie-sitting gig was more boring than I'd feared. At least I had the date to look forward to, though the more I thought about paintballing, the less I wanted to go. The last time Ian was around his basketball buddies, he'd been as communicative as a house plant. Regression would be bad.

And really, how much fun could shooting *fake* guns at people be?

"EAT PAINT, ASS MONKEYS!"

It was a glorious moment, the crowning achievement of my seventeen years of existence. There I was, sporting no paint splatters myself, systematically sniping each of Ian's unsuspecting teammates off of the field. I also screamed *a lot* of obscenities. Like, *all* the obscenities. I'm not sure Ian warned them that he dated a hunter, but I was pretty sure they figured it out quickly enough.

When Julie and I showed up—her in a pink sweat suit that would be decimated in no time flat, me in military-issued fatigue pants, a black sweatshirt, and my combat boots—a few of the guys 'warned' us that getting hit with paintballs hurt. One of them suggested that we should sit out and watch a round to be 'sure we wanted to play.' His name was Aaron. I didn't like Aaron. It's why every game, regardless of who was closest by, I hunted him down and pinged him right off the bat. The first time I got his shoulder, which was satisfying because the paint splatters got in his mouth. The second time it was his thigh, precariously close to his nuts. The third time, this game, I sniped him in the butt. He grabbed onto his bum like he'd pooped himself and shouted "Deadman!" as he slinked towards the safety cage.

Paintball was fast becoming my new favorite thing in the world. Ian was my team captain. At first he tried to give me a few hints on how to win, but after I nailed three guys from the other team right off the bat, he let me do my thing. Julie wasn't playing anymore; she got nailed in the boob within the first fifteen minutes and got a doozy of a bruise, so she sat on the bench and watched everyone else, acting as a makeshift cheerleader. Occasionally she'd root for her boyfriend, who was on the opposite team, or give a shout out for me or Ian. Otherwise she fondled her chest and grimaced a lot. To be fair, it looked like it had hurt.

Ian didn't do too badly for himself, though he got out early in the third round. We played thirty minute matches, and this one was last man standing. Teams no longer mattered, it was every man for himself. I'd only seen one other guy left—the captain of the basketball team who'd given Ian the shot at the party—but I could *hear* someone scuffling to my right. I counted on sound more than anything, something Mom taught me a long time ago. Some vampires could turn into mist or shadows, which meant they had no bodily form to track, so you had to hear the whisper of their movements. The guy closest to me thought he was quiet. He was as subtle as a fart in church.

I waited for my opportunity to strike, patience being a virtue and all that crap. Eventually, he got restless, and I heard him sliding over the concrete. A feral grin oozed across my mouth. He was coming, and I waited for him like a viper. It was a matter of time.

There was a thud, a soft sigh, and he emerged from behind his barricade. I lifted my gun, taking aim right as his hand came over the upper edge of the concrete. *BAM!* I nailed him, hitting him on the index and middle fingers. He yelped and twisted around in a circle, shaking the sting from his hand. I almost cackled aloud, but that would have given me away to Mark, Ian's team captain, so I bit my lip and grinned instead.

"Deadman," the guy I'd hit announced. "Ian, stop letting your girlfriend beat us up, dude. She's Robocop over here."

I could hear Ian laughing from the cage. "She's awesome."

The praise made me blush.

I rolled onto my stomach, crawling across the dirty ground to get to the back corner. Mark would have to move sooner or later, otherwise the match would be a draw, and I'm pretty sure he took my flawless victories as an affront to men everywhere. His expression after I nailed him in the hip with a paintball during the second match suggested as much, anyway.

Unlike the other guy, he stayed quiet. So quiet, I couldn't figure out exactly where he hid, which meant I'd have to lure him out. I looked around for something to throw: a rock, a piece of concrete block, the body of a hapless paintball victim. I came up short, though, and so I did what any good hunter would do. I played dirty. I took off my boot and tossed it at a threesome of construction barrels twenty feet to my right. I wanted him to think I was over there, and the only way to do that was to make a ruckus. In the meanwhile, I kept my head low and edged around the corner, my gun drawn and ready.

It was too easy. Mark slid out from behind some pallets to run at the barrels, his gun drawn and ready. He wasn't close enough yet, so I cocked my rifle and breathed slow, waiting for him to come into perfect snipe position. He mad-dashed, spraying everything around him in bright orange paint. It was so willy-nilly I almost laughed, but I managed to hold back. Especially when I pulled the trigger and nailed him in the shoulder with a splash of blue paint.

"Shit! Shit! Deadman. Shit!"

I surfaced from my hidey-hole to grin, trying to look normal despite my lack of boot making me totter like Quasimodo.

"Good game," I said, leaning over the barrel to retrieve my shoe.

"Yeah, GG. You're a beast with a gun. For serious."

"Thanks."

He shook his head and made for the bench. Julie hooted and hollered at me, shaking a section of chain fence while she jumped up and down with excitement. I waved at her as I wedged my foot back into my boot. Ian jogged out to join me in the arena, a huge grin splitting his face. I played it cool, like I wasn't bursting at the seams with my awesomeness. But let's be honest—I was spectacularly awesome and both of us knew it.

"Nice," he said, holding my gun so I could lace my boot.

"Thanks." As soon as I stood again, he leaned in for a celebratory kiss. It wasn't a quick brush of lips either. It was a 'cling to his shirt and close my eyes' type of kiss. My arms wrapped around the back of his neck, sliding through a slippery patch of paint. He squatted, grabbing me underneath my thighs and foisting me. The next thing I knew I was suspended off the ground. My eyes flew open, and I laughed against his mouth. This was one of the last things I expected from a guy so shy in public he could only manage one word answers. He laughed back and gave me another kiss, which promptly stifled any of my smart-ass commentary.

Not that I had much to say because it was pretty much the best thing ever.

*   *   *

WE PARTED WAYS with his crew at nine. Julie and John went back to John's house, and Ian agreed to come back to mine after I promised Janice would be wearing pants.

"Rotter boyfriend is probably there. You've been forewarned," I said as we headed to his car. We'd changed into normal people clothes before leaving the building so we wouldn't get paint on his dad's leather upholstery. I wanted to gloat and point out that *I* wouldn't have made a mess anyway, because *I* was splen-fucking-diferous and clean as a whistle, but I bit it back and smiled a lot instead. I didn't want to make Ian think I was an egotistical hag who hated his friends, even if the egotistical hag part was true.

"It's cool. I've never met a real vampire before, and uhh— the other night wasn't a 'meeting'." A crooked smile played around his mouth. "More like 'show and tell'."

I smirked. "Hardy harr. I'd never met one either, so it was a first for me, too. Oh, right. Our pet zombie is there now, too. I should mention that so you don't freak out when you see her."

Apparently, that one wasn't as cool, because he stopped pulling out of the parking lot to give me a look that suggested I'd lost my mind. My statement probably painted a picture of a slathering shambler tied up to a chain and living in a doghouse in my backyard, so I made the necessary corrections, relaying Lauren's sad story and how Mom waited on the DoPR's verdict before doing anything. It must have been adequate clarification, because he eased the car onto the road, shaking his head the whole time.

"Man, that's so crazy," he said. "It's cool, but I can't imagine living that way. Like, my parents do some whacked out crap. My mom's in a Wiccan coven, and my dad's into purification fasting and eating grass, but you got me beat. Seriously."

I rolled the window down, turning my face into the warm breeze. The air smelled like fresh cut grass which, for reasons I never understood, made me happier than a pig in shit. I wanted to bottle up the smell and carry it with me all the time. It made me think of summer and ice cream and barbecued chicken—all things I was a fan of, the last two likely responsible for my wobbling arm flab. "It's not bad. Well, it's never boring anyway."

"Yeah. I guess that's true."

We drove in quiet for a while, pulling into my driveway twenty minutes later. I grabbed my bag of paintball clothes and walked around the front of the car to take Ian's offered hand. It was the first night the peepers wailed from behind my house, and I smiled at the thought that soon, Ian would be out of school and we might get to hang more. I hoped he wouldn't get his head on straight and realize he dated a girl with a screwed up life. I was pretty sure I'd miss him when he took off screaming.

"Did you want to head inside to see if she's naked?" Ian asked beneath his breath. I elbowed him and made for the porch, creating as much noise as possible as I stomped into the house. On the off chance Janice was doing something bizarre, like hanging from the ceiling or wearing a Hazmat suit, I'd at least telegraphed my arrival so she could, you know, stop and not embarrass me to death again.

The good news was she sat at the kitchen table waiting for us, looking for all intents and purposes like a mom ought to look. There was even a Betty Crocker thing going on thanks to a plate of homemade cookies. The vampire sitting to her left kind of killed the illusion, but this was a huge improvement over the other night. At least no one could see any flopping jangs.

"Hey, you two. How are you?" Mom asked.

"Pretty good."

"Good. I sent Lauren downstairs. She wasn't comfortable seeing people yet, but she sends her best. And Ian, I'm sorry about the other night. It was..." Mom's face turned pink, and Jeff squeezed her shoulder. My fingers tingled with the desire to brush him away from her, but I shoved my hands into my pockets. I hadn't made nice-nice about vampire boyfriend only to ruin it by being over-protective now.

Mom sighed. "It wasn't good. I'm sorry. It's a bad first impression."

Ian shrugged and tried to play it cool, though I noticed the tops of his ears turning red. "It's okay."

"Good."

She smiled, he smiled, I smiled, we all smiled, and I made the mistake of assuming that meant everything was copacetic. I thought that Mom and Ian had made peace, that I was improving by not wanting to stake Jeff. I told myself that for once, tonight would go perfectly, that the paintball was the beginning, and that I could go upstairs and hang with Ian and it'd be awesome. Even if The Sex wasn't on the docket, I was happy to have him around. He was nice to me and made me think that my quirks were interesting instead of freakish.

Yeah, I thought it'd be a fantastic date night with a fantastic ending. I got so far as to take Ian's arm and to pull him towards the stairs.

And then my mom ruined everything by throwing acid in my face.

CHAPTER FOURTEEN

MY FACE BURNED, my eyes burned; it was like she'd dunked my head in a vat of fryer grease. I wheezed and backed away, hitting the wall hard, a picture behind me rattling and threatening to topple. That didn't stop me from thrashing like I was on fire. I tripped and stumbled around like I could outrun the pain. Strong arms wrapped around my upper body, hefting me off of the floor. I didn't know who it was, I didn't care who it was. I thrashed, keening all the while. I was in so much agony that it didn't immediately occur to me that another date night had essentially gone to Hell and back again.

"Maggie. Margaret. Listen to me."

Mom's voice penetrated, but only because the pain downgraded from 'red hot lava in eyes' to 'boiling hot water in eyes.' My nerve endings pulsed like they wanted to burst through my skin. I tried talking through it, to ask what happened, but I wasn't coherent. I did manage to lump a bunch of swears together to form one long, never-ending obscenity, though. If the *Guinness Book of World Records* caught wind of it, they'd clock me in for 'Longest, Rudest Rant in the History of Man.' In my defense, I felt like I was being eaten alive at the time, so it was justified.

"Maggie, listen. I'm sorry. Ian, sit down? Have a cookie or... shit me. I'll explain, I promise. Jeff, bring her this way?"

Wait, what? I was held by a *vampire*?

My panic-stricken brain latched onto that like a wood tick on a labradoodle. Flashbacks of my interlude with Ahmad and Lubov made me scream aloud, though this time not in pain. This was fury that a rotter manhandled mer for a second time in two days. This wasn't acceptable; I didn't want to be touched. He needed to get his dirty, stinking corpse hands off of me or so help me, I'd sever them off at the wrists.

"LET GO OF ME, YOU FANGED FREAK."

He didn't let go, not when I kicked my sneaker back at his knee to take out his legs. I could hear Ian shouting something at my mother and her shouting back, but I was in such a fit trying to get away from Jeff I couldn't follow their conversation. My feet made contact with Jeff's leg again and again, a picture perfect execution of Janice's 'what to do when you've been grabbed' lessons. He sighed, moving me back towards the kitchen, making sure he pointed my flailing in such a way that I wouldn't destroy my house. I forced my eyes open despite feeling like I'd been shot in the face with lightning. Everything was hazy and blurry, the light on the ceiling looking more like a sun than a halogen bulb.

"M-Mom, make him... Mom!"

"I'm here. Set her down and let her go. I'm here. I swear she'll be fine, Ian. It's okay." Jeff deposited me into a chair and those tight, strong arms moved away from me. I forced myself to relax, no longer frenzying that vampire-boyfriend had his mitts on me. I breathed so heavily I sounded like I hyperventilated, but it helped keep the panic at bay, it helped keep me centered. I blinked to bring the room into the focus, but the colors around me bled together, like I looked at the world through a Monet painting, or maybe a kaleidoscope. I touched my face to feel if I was maimed as surely something that burned that much had to have ruined me for life. My skin was warm to the touch and covered with tear tracks, but it felt whole and unscarred.

"Maggie." Mom moved closer to me, a human-shaped blob of pinks and peaches and blues. Her hands found mine, and she squeezed my fingers. "I'm sorry I hurt you, but it's important."

"Why? Why'd you do that?" I asked, my voice cracking halfway through. It finally registered that Ian had watched this whole thing, had seen me freaking out like a swearing, spitting lunatic girl. I'd calmed, could think straight again, but that didn't make it better. "I... Ian, I'm sorry. Oh, God."

"It's okay," Ian said. "Are you okay? Is she okay? She's red. Should we take her to the hospital?"

"No. She'll be okay. It's holy water. Maggie, listen to me. You've been ghouled."

It would have been kinder to run me over with the van. I felt like all the air had been knocked out of me, like she'd clobbered me so hard I saw stars. There was no way I could be a ghoul. Lubov and Ahmed were Max's ghouls, and they'd had super speed and super strength because of it. I couldn't do anything cool. I'd been paintballing all night, and not once did I get super reflexes or killer hearing. The only weird thing going on was the insomnia and sniffing thing, and if those were ghoul perks, they were crappy ones. Besides, Max hadn't done anything to me. We'd talked, and he'd warned me off of telling Mom, but that was it.

Ghouling someone *had* to take more than witnessing bad yoga moves and sitting on a couch. It had to.

"No. You're wrong."

Mom kept talking like she hadn't heard me. "When were you taken? Was it at night? Or during the day when I was at work? It was what, two days ago?"

Answering questions was instinctual, especially when it was your mother asking, so I tried to explain. Next thing I knew, the whole throbbing-face-thing was joined by horrible retching noises erupting from the back of my throat. I grabbed my neck and wheezed, squeezing my eyes closed as I fought for air. Of course, I couldn't tell her, because that went against Max's rules. Gagging fits were my friendly reminder of Max's rules.

"She can't say," I heard Jeff say. "If she was told not to tell anyone, ghouls can't betray a master's command. It's the nature of the bond."

"She can't say anything? Breathe, Maggie. Breathe."

"No."

"Can she nod yes or no answers?"

"Probably not."

"Not a..." I rasped through attempts to swallow air. "M'fine."

"No, you're not fine. You're not sleeping or eating, and you sniffed out Lauren. The holy water burned you. You're ghouled, Margaret. I'm sorry." Mom released me. I saw her reaching across the table. There was a snap and a chewing noise a moment later, and I knew she mowed down on nicotine gum. If there'd been a pack of cigarettes around, she'd have been smoking them one after another despite being butt-free for the better part of five years. "She's not contagious or anything, Ian. You can come over. There's nothing to worry about."

"Uhh. All right?"

"Let him go home," I said, silently adding *so he can never call me again*. There was no way he'd be okay with this one. Hell, I wasn't okay with this. Me, Maggie Cunningham, a hunter AND a ghoul. How could this happen? This had to be karma in action. Some god somewhere was mad I'd worn the Snooki bras and saw fit to punish me for my fashion offenses.

"It's okay, Mags. I'll stay. Is there anything I can do?"

"Get her a bottle of water."

Blurs and slashes of colors passed me by, everyone moving around the kitchen in a nervous dance. I squinted. My eyes watered so much it probably looked like I'd never stopped crying, but the pain was more tolerable. Agony had become hurt, hurt had become discomfort. Maybe in a few minutes discomfort would downgrade to annoyance.

"It has to be related to the Plasma kill," Mom said, though she seemed to be talking to herself more than me. "Retribution for that fledgling. I hate vampire politics. It's a bunch of juvenile bullshit. Stupid fangers. No insult intended."

Jeff chuckled from somewhere behind me. "None taken. If it's any consolation, a singular dose will wear off, though it can take some time if the vampire's old."

"Don't talk about me like I'm not here," I demanded, not bothering with the whole 'be nice to Mommy's dead boyfriend' thing.

"What's a dose?" Ian asked at the same time.

"Blood. A blood dose."

I wanted to point at Jeff and say, "Ha, I didn't drink his blood so I couldn't be ghouled!" I hadn't sucked on his neck or chewed on his finger. But then I remembered Lubov pouring me the Coke in that funky glass. I'd looked at the bottom of it and I'd seen nothing, but the upper half had been all of those pretty colors. If they'd planned ahead of time, if they figured I'd be suspicious of them and they needed to keep me quiet, they could have laced it before I'd arrived. They could have smeared his blood...

Oh gross. Just *gross*.

Ian plunked down in the chair across from me, a bottle of water in hand. He slid it across the table, his fingers brushing over mine for a stolen second. I tried to smile, but my face was so swollen it probably made me look I had to fart. "I'm sorry. Again. I didn't know," I said.

"No, it's... man. Are you okay?"

"Yeah. It doesn't hurt that much anymore."

Mom paced back and forth between the fridge and the stove, murmuring under her breath and slapping the countertop every couple seconds. By her growls and twitches, I could tell she was close to a Terminator-With-Tatas rampage. Considering me and Ian were human, I was pretty sure we were safe from misdirected anger. The vampire and the zombie, though, well...

They might have it rough.

"Tomorrow that scientist is coming from DoPR about Lauren, so I can't do anything until *that's* over. Some asshole messes with my kid and she can't tell me who, and I can't go snooping around until what, Thursday? Friday if this zombie thing goes long? By then it could be too late. By then..."

"It's all right, Janice," Jeff interjected. He moved across the kitchen to wrap his arms around her from behind. Seeing it, or quasi-seeing it as the case may be, made me flinch. "You'll find them. It's not like you have to rush. Vampires are too arrogant to run away from a human, regardless of her station." He nuzzled at her ear, and she slipped her hand back over her shoulder to touch his cheek.

That was all I could take of *that*. The ghouling thing was bad enough. Watching them be all grabby sweet was the poop frosting on my turd cake.

I stood up so fast the kitchen chair skittered across the floor tiles behind me. "Are you done throwing shit at me? If so, I'd like to go upstairs and be pissy now."

"You're off the hook," Mom said. "Sorry about the holy water. I'm so pissed off right now I can't think straight." She looked over at Ian, casting him a tight, pained smile. "I swear I'm not the world's worst mother. I just look like it sometimes. A lot lately. I'm sorry. Again."

"No. No, I didn't think... " He didn't finish the sentence because I took his hand and yanked him towards the stairs. I knew Mom was having another one of those 'feel bad about being a weirdo Mom' moments, but I was in no condition to feel sorry for her right now. I was too busy feeling sorry for myself, and Ian was there for me, not her. She'd have to be content with her vampire hump boy's reassurances.

If that wasn't enough for her, too bad.

WE GOT HALFWAY up the steps before I remembered the disaster that was my bedroom. It looked like a tornado hit it, complete with clothes hanging from drawers, sheets and blankets everywhere, and stacks of clutter covering my desk and vanity. That wasn't taking into account the arsenal lying around: knives, stakes, guns. I had one of every dangerous thing in existence somewhere on my floor. All I needed was a T-Rex and my death trap was complete.

"So my room's a mess," I said. "Don't touch anything and watch where you step. I'll... yeah. I need to move the machete."

"The what?"

"Nothing."

I opened the door and pretended living in near-quarantined conditions was no big deal. Ian followed me, picking his way around the various piles of crap to claim a corner of the bed. I did a cursory sweep, making sure all firearms and pointies got put into the closet before they blew off feet or faces. I picked up laundry, too, stuffing it into the hamper.

"You don't have to clean up for me. It's cool."

"I don't..." I sighed and turned to smile at him. "I don't think I care that it's dirty. I don't know what to do right now, you know? Trying to distract myself." I moved over to the mirror to inspect my face, confirming my earlier assertion that I was not, in fact, sporting burns or scars. I looked pink and sweaty, but otherwise fine.

"Can I ask you something?"

I glanced at him in our reflection. "Sure."

"If I hadn't passed out the other night, would this have happened to you?"

I turned around to stare at him, like in the span of a single sentence he'd gone from Ian-my-date to Ian-the-carnival-freak. He couldn't blame himself for this. He couldn't. That was way too... nice? Aware? Hell, I hadn't thought of it, and I was the one magically tethered to some vampire in Boston. I *should* be looking for people to blame, and Ian's tangential part in things never occurred to me.

"No!"

"Your mom said it was related to the Plasma thing, which only happened because you're a virgin." He looked down at his hands. "And I mean, you wouldn't be if..."

"Ian, no. No, no, no." I sat beside him on the bed. He wouldn't look at me, so I grabbed his chin to turn his face my way.

It's okay, he didn't need that neck. He'd grow another one.

"Look, shit happens, and it happened at the party. We've been good since then, though, right? I think you're crazy for sticking around, but I'm happy you do. And I don't expect you to, like, slip me the dong out of duty. Rather you wanted to than felt you had to."

"Oh, I want to."

He put so much emphasis on the 'want' that my face went hot again, but this time it had nothing to do with the holy water. He cleared his throat. "I wanted to, you know, make it up to you after the party. This whole thing has been strained 'cause you need to do it for work but I didn't want you to think that's all I'm around for. I have fun. Tonight was fun. You do cool stuff, and I like hearing you talk about your job. It's... you're not dead, right? Ghouls aren't dead?"

I smiled like an idiot because he said so many good things, so many right things. My stomach flopped around, my chest tightened. I crushed so hard on him right then that I completely missed his question about the dead thing until he repeated it a minute later. Twice.

"Dead? No. No!"

"Oh. I don't know what a ghoul is, so I wasn't sure."

"I'm human. I'm alive." I wanted to say more, to explain so everything made sense to him, but I was so fearful of another gagging fit, I stopped myself. I couldn't tell him I was someone's magical pet. I couldn't say that even though it was a temporary condition, I felt dirty, like I should scrub my skin raw to get the vamp cooties off. Maybe it was for the best. Ian'd seen enough bizarro-world already. I worried

I'd lose him if I heaped much more onto his pile. Too many details could break his brain and make him give up for good.

He lugged me into his side, pressing his nose into my hair. I slumped against him, taking his hand and pulling it into my lap. We didn't say anything for a few minutes, letting the silence speak to all of the things we couldn't or didn't want to give voice to, but after a while he lifted my chin and kissed me. It wasn't anything sexy, not like The Sex kisses from the party, but it was nice all the same. I nudged at his lips with mine, toying with the hair at his nape. He looked at me, I looked at him, and before I knew better, I climbed over his lap, my knees dropping to the outsides of his thighs.

Screw it. Game face on.

"Let's do it. Not because of work, but 'cause we can."

"You're sure?" He ran his hands down my sides, sending a shiver rippling down my spine. "I don't want you to think... "

"Less thinky. More fucky," I said, my fingers fumbling with the buttons on my shirt. He kissed me again, this time harder and more insistent, his tongue flicking at mine before pulling away. I groaned in protest, wanting to demand that he cut the crap and do proper make-outs like *a real man*, but then he grinned against my mouth.

"You're awesome, Mags."

I'd have told him I knew it, maybe said something glib and witty, but he tugged up my shirt and licked over my stomach, and all thought promptly flew out the window.

CHAPTER FIFTEEN

I WAS PRETTY sure I had reasonable expectations for The Sex, Round Two. I'd gotten an idea of what Ian was like from the party, and for all that things went askew towards the end, I'd enjoyed ninety percent of the precursors. Sure, he attacked my girl bits with the fury of a thousand suns, but he meant well when he did it. At least, I had to assume he did, otherwise he had some serious vagina rage I didn't want to think about.

Boy, was I in for a treat, and by treat I mean an orgasm. Like a real one, not one of the practice runs done in the privacy of my room. The differences between a drunk Ian and a cognizant Ian were night and day. What felt good before—the kisses and touches and nuzzles and licks—were so much better when he was aware of how his actions affected my body. Like, instead of taking my invitation to screw as a reason to toss my legs over my head and have at me, he kissed me for what felt like hours. His mouth nudged at mine, tongue flicking out to tease my lips before pulling away. He got me so eager to make out I wanted to yank his ears off his skull and scream at him to stop wasting time. I didn't because that wouldn't be very gracious and I was all about being a lady and shit, but I did make impatient sighing noises and tug on the ends of his hair. He had the audacity to smile at me before giving me what I wanted, which was the type of lingering kiss that curled toes and made me groan in the back of my throat.

My eyes closed, my arms slid over his shoulders. His hands ran down my back, fingers looping under the bottom of my shirt. He pulled away from me to yank it up, ignoring the buttons in front and going for the clean strip. I lifted my arms, my eyes skittering over to the light switch on the wall. I didn't want the light on anymore. It wasn't that I didn't want to see him, it was that I didn't want him to see me, not sitting in his lap like this. Flab squished out over the top of my jeans and I had those weird wing things under my arms.

"The light."

"Mmm?" He threw the shirt onto the floor, his mouth finding the side of my neck and nibbling. My palms flattened against his chest, and I shoved so I could lean past him to flick the switch. For good measure, I also locked my door and put on the radio.

"Why'd you do that? I like looking at you."

"'Cause I'm squishy."

"It's a good squishy." I'd have argued, but his hands squeezed my bum and he rotated around so he could lower me down onto my bed. I shoved a book, a *Cosmopolitan* magazine, and a sweatshirt to the floor so I could lay flat beneath him. My mattress had become a raft floating in an endless sea of crap. "Shoulder's okay?" He asked as he kissed over my bra, his fingers sliding around back to unlatch the clasp. He fumbled with it some, jerking at the hooks hard enough to bend them. Eventually, they came free, though whether it was because he got them properly unhitched or because he ripped them out, I didn't know.

"Y... shit. Yeah." I felt the satin sliding off of my skin, exposing my chest completely. We hadn't done this at his house last week; we'd kept my bra on, so this was a new experience, and with all new experiences, it was freaky. I had big boobs, which was good on one hand, bad on the other, namely because the weight of my boobs made them ooze their way towards my armpits. I'd seen the movies—women on their backs should have boobs pointed at a ninety-degree angle at all times. We weren't supposed to go floppy and spready. Gravity wasn't supposed to do its gravity thing.

Gravity sucked. Fuck gravity.

"I'm sorry I'm..."

I didn't get to finish the sentence because there were hands squeezing and kneading and lifting and then a mouth was sucking. I was afraid Ian'd be poking me and snickering that I'd gone all floppy on him, but no, he seemed utterly oblivious to the migratory pattern of Maggie's boobs. And because he wasn't hung up on it, I couldn't be hung up on it either. I was too preoccupied with the happy tingles to worry about the interstate running between my cleavage.

"Oh, tha... nngh."

Words failed, moans did not. In fact I did a lot of moaning then—quietly, of course, because the last thing I wanted was for my mom and her boyfriend to clue in to what we did, but that's what the radio was for. I was thankful for it, even if it played a commercial for a plumbing company when I got my freak on with my boyfriend. Nothing says loving like poop chutes and drain clogs.

Ian worked his way from my chest to my stomach, and I was reminded of his drunken girl belly ramblings from the party. It made me grin in the dark, and I put a hand on his head, my thumb stroking over his brow. He pulled back and I heard some shuffling, then he climbed up over me to give me another kiss. His bare chest met mine, and I ran my fingers down the warm skin of his back. I liked how this felt, his weight on me. I liked that from our mouths to our bellybuttons were sealed tight against one another, like you didn't know where one body started and the other ended. It felt intimate. It felt good. It made me make growly noises I equated with livestock.

We kissed until I needed to come up for air, and I pulled back to pant into the dark. He kissed my neck, my ear, and my shoulder. I heard the jingle of his keys as he pulled off his pants. I took that as my cue to do the same, and my hands went to my waist band, shaking so badly I feared I couldn't manage a simple thing like a zipper. I wasn't scared so much as tense. This part we'd done before, this part I knew. He hadn't died of shock and horror the last time he'd touched my bits; I was pretty sure he wouldn't this time either.

I shucked the undies with the pants, dumping the whole lot onto the floor and waiting for Ian to do something interesting. He may have only been with one other girl before, but that was one more person than I'd been with, which meant until I had my bearings with this whole sticky thing he was the ringleader. I couldn't see much in the dark of my room, so I had to rely on my hearing to figure out what he did. I heard fumbling, a tearing sound, and then a murmured curse.

Swearing while putting on a condom wasn't a good sign. I made a vow then and there that if another attempt at The Sex went wrong, I was forsaking men and hunting and joining a convent because God clearly didn't want me to get laid. I'd be the surliest, most foul-mouthed nun ever, but that's what He got for ruining this for me.

"Everything all right down there?"

"Yeah. Can't see a damned thing. It's good now."

"Did you miss your dick?"

"... no."

"Oh. Good."

His hands went to my legs, running up to my knees, and I felt him kissing my hip. I idly wondered if that's because he missed my stomach, but no, he seemed perfectly content pressing his face against my side as he touched my thighs. I braced, waiting for him to pound his fingers against me until I begged for mercy, but again, the difference between drunk Ian and not-drunk Ian was overwhelming. He didn't push and mash and stab at me. He took his time, stroked, and the moment I made a squealy noise because he did it right, he kept doing it that same way. Over and over. Back and forth. And when I breathed heavier and faster, and my fingers fisted in the sheets at my side and the muscles in my legs flexed and my toes pointed at the wall, he sped up, matching the pace my body set.

And then it was there. The perfect moment—the hard pulses and the shuddering breaths and the head thrashing back and forth. I'd like to say I said something eloquent then, maybe something mushy and romantic in appreciation of the totally-unexpected-yet-utterly-awesome-orgasm, but the best I could manage was a loud, half chicken squawked, "FUCK YES." Ian didn't seem to mind my outburst, though; he ran his hand up and down my body and let me ride out the waves.

It would have been nice to sit there and drool over what happened, maybe make happy noises and gurgle until the aftershocks went away, but Ian kissed my stomach and moved over me, nuzzling at my neck and reminding me that 'oh yeah, he has a boner and wants to use it.' My arms wrapped around him and squeezed him tight, my mouth skimmed over his cheek in invitation to finish what we started. Everything was good, everything was perfect. I was so very glad I was with this guy here and now.

But then he said, "You're wet" right into my ear, and the perfect STUFF went right out the window. It's not that I didn't expect it as a side effect of what we'd done, it's just I didn't want to think about it. It seemed unsanitary, like mentioning those burps where you taste puke in your mouth.

"Ugh! I'm sorry!"

"I love it. It's hot," he said, and I felt him shift and press up against me. It was hot? News to me—I thought it was bogus—but I wasn't given long to mull it over. We were almost there, almost at the moment where I'd go from 'Maggie Cunningham, Vampire Bait' to 'Maggie Cunningham, Punching Vampires in the Spleen,' but oddly, none of that occurred to me. All that mattered was Ian being there with me, that Ian kissed me, that Ian held me, that Ian...

Did me. Oh. Right.

He went slow, which was appreciated, but it didn't change the fact that he was a girthy guy and I was tight. There was a bit of discomfort, which became a bit more discomfort when he surged ahead. I felt a twinge, a sharp pain that abated immediately, and he paused. He nuzzled at my neck, breathing heavily into my ear.

"Tell m-me when it's okay to go."

I wasn't sure what that meant. It was good to go now, wasn't it? Sure, there'd been some ouch factor involved, but that was expected. He hadn't mauled me from bellybutton to knee with his penis. I mean, he was decent sized, but it wasn't like he impaled me with Dick-O-Tron over here. Getting the glass gouge in my shoulder had hurt way more than anything he'd done.

"Uhh. Go for it."

He moved, capturing my mouth in another kiss as he worked faster and harder. It chafed, even with that wet he'd been rude enough to mention, but I didn't have to bear it long. A minute or two later he went rigid, yelped into my mouth, and buried himself deep, going very, very still and slumping on top of me. I'd read a bunch of *Cosmo* articles about women who wanted their guys to last forever, but I was glad he finished. I'd had fun up to the actual sex part of things, and I figured eventually I might want the whole kit and caboodle for hours, but not this time. This time I wanted to curl up next to him and bask in the knowledge that not only had we gotten the deed done, we'd done it well.

DESPITE MY INSOMNIAC tendencies, I dozed off for about an hour, content to lie around and be lazy. I woke when Ian kissed my shoulder and sat up, trying to sneak around in the dark to get his clothes. He hissed as he stubbed his toe on a random piece of furniture.

"I'll get the light."

"Thanks. I got my boxers and pants, but my shirt's, like, gone."

I wrapped myself up in a blanket and flicked on the switch, having to blink for a good minute to adjust. He found his shirt draped over the stereo and tugged it over his head, turning to look at me with a smile. He crawled across the bed to give me a kiss, his fingers skimming over my cheek. "You're pretty."

My eyes swept to the vanity and I snorted. I was as pink as a pork chop thanks to the holy water splash, I had major bedhead, and my 'clothes' consisted of a comforter riddled with holes and an unidentifiable oily stain along the top. Oh yeah, I screamed sexpot.

"Uh huh."

He grinned and donned his shoes. "I gotta head home before my 'rents freak out. You got plans Friday?"

"Probably not. I doubt my mom's going to take me on any hunts 'til this ghoul thing is over." Didn't that figure; I'd finally slept with someone for my journeyman license, and I'd be sitting around waiting for Max's blood tag to run its course before I could do squat. It should have pissed me off a lot more than it did, but I guess I was so stoked from getting my bang on with Ian I couldn't muster much in the way of irritation. Maybe this was that silly afterglow thing I'd read about.

"Cool. I'll call Jules. We'll hook up. Maybe a movie?"

"Sure, okay."

He finished lacing up his sneakers and patted his pockets for his keys. I pulled on a pair of sweatpants and a tank top before combing my hair. Mom would catch on to my outfit change, but there was no way I'd make Ian head downstairs alone, even if that meant risking a smart-ass Janice comment. He was probably terrified of her, or assumed she was a psycho slut from Hell. I couldn't blame him for either; the first time he saw her she was bare-assed and riding a dead guy. This time she burned his sort-of-girlfriend with holy water. I didn't have time to do it before he left, but I wanted to talk to him about Mom. I loved her even if she did things that made me want to rub my face with a cheese grater. I didn't want him ragging on her or getting the wrong idea.

She was important to me, freakish tendencies and all. Ian and I had gotten a do-over. Maybe Ian and Mom could have one, too.

"Hey, Friday why don't you and me go out?" I blurted. He probably figured I meant for The Sex, but whatever. It wasn't like I was against the idea. "Maybe we can do something with Julie and John Saturday? I mean, if you want to hang Saturday. I don't know your schedule."

"Sure. That sounds good."

"Cool." I rolled off the bed and opened my door, leading him down to the living room. The television blazed, and I took Ian's hand, giving him a reassuring squeeze as we approached. Mom cuddled on the couch with Jeff, still looking like a Mommy Murder Machine. A petty part of me wished Jeff would accidentally piss her off and she'd stake him through the forehead.

Once we'd hit the foot of the stairs, Mom glanced up. I felt my spine go stiff when she looked at me, and I waited for her to say something that'd make me want to flush my head in the toilet. I didn't know if it was her crappy mood or the desperate expression on my face, but she kept her mouth closed, her attention drifting to Ian. She forced a smile for his sake and sat up straighter.

"Drive safe, and maybe next time I see you it'll be under better circumstances. G'night, kiddo."

"Yeah, thanks," Ian said, though I wasn't sure what he thanked her for. It's not like she'd done anything normal since he'd met her. "See you soon."

"Good night," Jeff said, and Ian was polite enough—or scared enough—to wave goodbye to him.

I led him to the driveway before anything could go wrong; I didn't have a lot of faith in life staying normal. Ian opened the driver's side door and pulled me into another hug, his lips brushing over the top of my ear. "It was okay?" he asked, and though he tried to play it cool, I could tell he needed reassurance that no, he hadn't turned me off from men forever, and no, I didn't want to hose myself down while screaming "Unclean!"

I gave him a gentle squeeze, my nose nuzzling at where the 58 was tattooed into his shoulder. "It was awesome. Ten stars out of ten. Would highly recommend." He laughed, and I pulled back to smile at him. "Thanks for putting up with all my crazy crap. Seriously."

"Nah, it's cool." He gave me another kiss, and when I felt my head spinning from lack of oxygen, I pulled away so he could climb into his car.

"Call me this week. I'm always around after nine," he said.

"'Kay."

I watched his rear lights disappear down the street. I wasn't tired thanks to the ghouling, but I wanted to get back into bed anyway, to rest and veg and not have to think about anything other than the good parts of my night. Tomorrow was soon enough to figure out my Janice problems. I headed inside, feeling Mom's eyes on me as I scampered through the living room and towards the stairs. I went fast enough to leave fire tracks in my wake, but she didn't point it out, nor did she ask any embarrassing questions. It was like, for once, she understood I needed to be left alone. It was like, for once, she got me.

Her timing had never been better.

CHAPTER SIXTEEN

I STAYED IN my room the rest of the night, napping when boredom got the better of me. I didn't want to go downstairs and answer embarrassing questions about my sparkly new sex life, nor did I want to deal with Jeff-The-Magic-Vampire, so I holed up in my dungeon. When I ran out of weapons to clean, I picked up my floor, managing to stuff half of the crap in trash bags. Ian had a far better chance of survival next visit thanks to my labors.

It wasn't until the next morning, when my mother rode the vacuum around the house like the Wicked Witch of Massachusetts, I bothered to surface. I opened my door, and was greeted by Mom in a pair of polka dotted underwear, an AC/DC tee shirt, and a pale green bandana wrapped over her hair.

"Hey. Did I wake you?" she shouted over the vacuum.

"I don't sleep. Ghoul, remember?"

I expected a smirk or a smart-ass reply, but she looked down, focusing on sucking up a dust bunny the size of an elephant. The hunting gig meant we were usually too busy for housekeeping, so we were behind on the whole tidiness thing. I couldn't blame Mom for straightening up; it'd be pretty embarrassing for the scientist coming from the DoPR to think we were scrubs. And who knew, maybe they'd take Lauren into protective custody for forcing her to live in a zombie ghetto, like the inch of dust on the baseboards meant we were awful foster-hunters and should hang our heads in shame.

I was about to ask what I could do to help around the house, but Lauren appeared at the foot of the stairs holding the recycling bin. She was dressed in the nicest of the Walmart outfits we'd bought, a white shirt and a pair of skinny jeans, and with her hair done up into a ponytail she looked startlingly alive. I couldn't smell grave stank wafting off of her anymore. There was a slight tang of chemical, but the sweet, meaty rot from before was all but gone. I didn't know what she'd done, maybe hosed herself down with Clorox or slept in the dishwasher, but it helped a ton.

"Do you put this on the curb, Janice?"

Mom shut off the vacuum and jiggled the cord to get it out of the electrical socket at the end of the hall. "Yeah. The garbage bins are by the porch if you want to pull them down to the end of the driveway. They do trash pick-up at noon."

"Okay."

Lauren took off. I could hear her making her way through the house towards the porch. For a skinny girl, she sure managed to sound like Godzilla tromping all over Tokyo. All we needed was a giant moth for her to battle in the front yard and we'd be set.

As soon as the side door slammed, Mom stopped what she was doing to look at me. "So how was it?"

"Huh?"

"With Ian. You okay?"

"Oh. That." My face went hot, like a mini version of last night's holy water burns. She knew what we'd done, there was no way she couldn't. If she hadn't guessed on her own by my clothes change, Jeff probably filled her in that 'Oh, by the way, I don't want to maul your flesh and blood for a virgin snack anymore.' Stupid vampire boyfriend with his stupid vampire senses. "Yeah. It was good."

She clapped me on the shoulder, a smile blooming on her mouth. "Welcome to the club of women who get to spend the next sixty years putting up with men's shit. There's no tee shirt, and the membership benefits are touch and go, but at least the sex is sometimes good and you get a journeyman license. As your mother I'm obligated to tell you to always wear a condom. And don't get crabs or gonoherpasyphilAIDS, or make me a grandmother before I'm fifty."

"Gono-what?"

"You know, gonorrhea, herpes, syphilis, and AIDS, but all mixed together into one huge STD."

"Gee, Mom. I don't plan on it. And yeah, we used a condom."

She patted my hair like I was seven. "Good kid. I knew I taught you something."

I was about to head downstairs to see if I could make heads or tails of the disaster area that was the kitchen (actually I wanted to escape the conversation about crotch disease) but Mom stopped me by tugging on the back of my tank top. She wrapped me in a fierce, rib-crushing hug, her face pressing against my shoulder. "I'm sorry about the ghouling. I should have known better than to try the Plasma thing. I fucked up and I'm sorry."

It was weird to go from joking about crabs to this, but life with Janice was always a roller coaster ride, and she pulled one-eighties far too often for me to be surprised by them anymore. "It's okay. I shouldn't have pushed and... I am okay. I am."

"No, you're not. Well you are, but you're not, and it sucks. I'll find them. I promise. I'll find them and ram it up their asses so hard they'll wish they'd never been un-deaded."

"NO." It was so loud, so emphatic she went stiff. What I wouldn't have given to be able to explain my gut-punch reaction. But I couldn't, and she knew it and I knew it, and so we were stuck with this loud, fierce denial that hung heavy on the air.

"I... right." She pulled away from me to wind the vacuum cord around her arm, her brow covered in worry lines. She tried so hard not to stress about it, yet it was written all over her face. I wanted to make it better, but I didn't have the faintest idea how.

Mom motioned at the steps. "Dr. Dempsey is going to be here in an hour and a half and we look like shit. Got to get the living room done and dust the dining room and take a shower and..."

"I've got the kitchen."

"Okay, good. Have Lauren help you with the dishes." She headed downstairs with the vacuum in tow. I called for her as she rounded the corner, and she paused on the landing.

I pointed at her butt. "You might want to put on pants before the doctor gets here."

The worry lines gave way to her lopsided smirk. "Nah. It's bribery. Impetus for him to see things my way."

"Or see your ass," I said. "'Cause I can when you bend over. You've got full plumber's crack going on."

She stooped to plug the vacuum into the wall, granting me an eyeful of said crack. I made a squick noise, but she ignored me, instead sizing up the dust bunnies on the floor like they were a sprite infestation. And much like a sprite infestation, those dust bunnies were going down. Mom was a hunter on a mission. "My way, my ass. Whatever." She grunted and turned on the vacuum. "Lately it's been the same thing anyway."

DR. DEMPSEY WAS a handsome man in his mid-fifties with a trim gray goatee and glasses. He looked like a black Mr. Rogers, with rich dark skin, an inviting smile, and a sweater-vest. I guess I expected some kind of *Duke Nukem* bad-ass with an Uzi ready to vanquish the zombie scum. What I got was a guy with a medical bag, a laptop, and a quiet voice. He sat in the living room with Lauren, checking her vitals—or lack thereof—conducting an interview, and typing things into his computer. Mom and I had been allowed in for the early stages of the visit, relaying what we saw in the park and Lauren's general demeanor since we'd housed her. But once that part was over, Dr. Dempsey wanted her alone. Mom and I made ourselves as scarce as our not-huge house allowed, but every once in a while we caught snippets of conversation. Sometimes it was about how Lauren felt, sometimes it was her instincts, sometimes it was, "What you remember from your death?"

None of it sounded particularly dour, but that didn't mean we were in the clear, and waiting for Dr. Dempsey's verdict was nerve wracking. I wasn't Lauren's closest friend or anything, but I thought she had a compelling case, and—in the vast scheme of the cosmos—she'd been handed a raw deal. Mom must have agreed. The half pack of Nicorette gone in under an hour was a bad sign.

"So what do you think?" I asked, watching Dr. Dempsey run Lauren through some drills to test her motor skills. He had her stand up, sit down, spin in circles, and touch her toes, all of which Lauren did perfectly well. She reacted like any normal person would.

"Don't know. He's not what I expected, but then the DoPR never is," Mom said. That was about as far as we got in our conversation, because Dr. Dempsey shook Lauren's hand and sent her out our way before calling for my mom. Mom took a deep breath and marched in, brushing elbows with Lauren as she passed. Lauren sat at the table across from me, immediately slumping into her seat and burying her face in her hands.

Crap. She was upset, which meant I'd have to do that empathy thing.

"Hey, uhh. How... are you?"

Lauren lifted her face to blink at me. "Dead and confused. He seems nice, but he said there wasn't any guarantee I wouldn't regress into a brain-chomping problem. I hope not, but..." She swallowed hard. "At least he has a theory on how it happened so maybe they can prevent it from happening to other people."

"Oh?"

"The radiation from my chemotherapy, the drugs I was on, magic in the area, and trace gamma something. I don't know. Something about the power plant. I don't understand the science, but basically my cells didn't die like they were supposed to." She forced a smile and reached for one of Mom's cookies. It was the first time I'd seen her eat something that hadn't formerly been alive. Apparently sugary, crappy food helped comfort zombies, too. "He said I was like the Incredible Hulk, just less green."

"Oh, wow. Well, maybe that'd explain your strength thing."
She snorted. "Maybe, though I don't think it's that literal."

Awkward silence shrouded the kitchen. Incredible Hulk jokes were easy but inappropriate, and "Aww it'll be okay" was inaccurate since none of us knew what Dr. Dempsey would decide. I looked over at the cookies, wishing I was hungry so I could commiserate with her over baked goods, but thanks to the ghouling I'd rather not eat at all. The only thing that truly interested me for food was meat.

"It's okay. Like, you don't have to try so hard with me," she said out of the blue. I cringed and looked up, hoping I didn't look as uncomfortable as I felt. I'd never developed a very good poker face in awkward situations.

"It's that obvious, huh?"

"Yeah. You look gassy whenever we talk."

A bubble of laughter escaped before I could think to squash it. Lauren smiled at me, popping her cookie into her mouth and glancing towards the living room. Mom and the doctor talked in hushed tones on the couch. Mom nodded a lot, but she didn't appear bummed. That was a good sign.

"I'm not good when people are upset," I said. "I feel like I'm bad at being sympathetic. I mean, I don't know how to... okay. What you're going through? I've got nothing that could compare, so it's hard to talk about it. This whole ghouling thing doesn't hold a candle."

Lauren nodded and sat back in her seat. "No, but your mom talked about it before you came home yesterday, to me and Jeff. She's worried. I hope you're okay."

I rolled my eyes up to the ceiling and shook my head. "Great. She tells one vampire about another vampire ghouling me. She might as well bring him with her to Boston to talk to the pri..."

My voice dropped like a rock when I realized what I was about to say. Talking about my kidnapping would make me choke like a dog on a chicken bone. Except, *it didn't.* I'd given a detail or two, yet there was no heave. I didn't understand it. Had the ghouling lost its effect already? If so, I still had no appetite, nor was I tired, so was it bits and pieces fading away? Or was Max too busy giving himself a Brazilian wax to keep his metaphysical strangle in place? He couldn't hold my voice captive consciously all the time— that'd take too much effort.

There was only one way to find out, and that was to make another stab at it. I wasn't overjoyed at the prospect, but what the hell was one more near-puking fit when you've already had three or four?

"I was ghouled by a prince named Max."

The words fell from my mouth all easy and smooth; the question was why? I thought back to what Jeff said to my mom last night in the kitchen after the holy water thing: "Ghouls can't betray a master's command." My master's command had been not to tell anyone, and I'd betrayed...

No, wait. My master's command was to not tell a living soul. A *living soul.* Lauren wasn't a living soul. She was a bona fide dead chick. She didn't fall into that gray area vampires did where they had pulses. She was animated dead—no heartbeat, no nothing.

Holy crap.

I grabbed her hand, staring at her like she'd become the center of the universe. Hopefully, Dr. Dempsey wasn't in the other room getting ready to *end* her universe, not only for her sake but for mine, too.

"Okay, listen. I need your help. I need to tell you what happened because I can. You're not... it doesn't matter why, but if I tell you, you can tell my mom, and can tell her not to... shit!" My sentences bumbled together, making me sound like a crazy person. I tried to breathe, to collect my thoughts. I needed to tell Lauren what happened with Max so she could relay it to my mother and—in turn—save my butt. Save Mom's butt. Whatever. I couldn't do any of it if I rambled.

Lauren peered at me, probably trying to figure out what the hell was wrong with my brain. "Are you okay, Maggie?"

It was the way she asked that took me off guard. It was soft and caring, like she truly gave a crap about my well-being. It snapped me out of my self-indulgent craze. I *was* okay. Her, not so much. Even if the DoPR gave her a pass, she might keep rotting. Dr. Dempsey might decide 'screw it' and tell Mom to end it now because the possibility of Lauren becoming a shambling nightmare was too great. He could sequester her in a lab for the rest of her unlife because she was a one-of-a-kind specimen.

This was the person asking *me* if *I* was okay. I should be asking after her, not the other way around.

I took a deep breath and swallowed hard. I would tell her about the Max thing later, after we found out what Dr. Dempsey thought. Until then, I needed to stop being a selfish turd. I slid my hand away from hers and went for the refrigerator, pulling out a big blob of red hamburger meat with my bare hands. I plopped it on a plate and brought it to the table, sliding it between us. Without thinking too much about how cold and icky it was, I grabbed a chunk and popped it in my mouth. It tasted coppery, but under the effects of the ghouling, I was a-okay with that. The meat thing was something I had in common with Lauren, and damn it, I would stop sucking and be supportive. We were going to bond if it killed us. Well, not her because she was already dead, but you get the gist.

Bonding. Over a heaping plate of dead cow.

"You know what, I'm fine. How are you doing?"

CHAPTER SEVENTEEN

"I SEE NO reason she can't continue on here, unless you think she's too dangerous for socialization or you can't house her any longer." Dr. Demspey packed up his computer at half past noon, smiling at all of us as he moved towards the door. Lauren waved at him. Lucky for her, he'd deemed her a non-threat, and by the grace of the United States government, she could let her zombie freak flag fly for the foreseeable future.

I hadn't gotten to tell my hamburger-chowing buddy about the prince thing yet because I was trying to listen more than talk during our kitchen stint. It was a learning experience for me in that whenever conversations got too serious, I tended to say smart-ass things to break the tension. Knowing Lauren awaited a potential death sentence tempered my funny; the more she talked about how sad the whole thing was, the less inclined I was to act out. This shit was kittens-in-the-rain depressing.

"If you want me to make more permanent arrangements, I can find a place for her at one of our facilities, but I'll need some time for that," Dr. Dempsey said. "I don't want to put her in a holding cell. They're suited for dangerous creatures, and she needs a dormitory, not lock-up."

Mom glanced at Lauren, then at me, and nodded. "It's all right that she stays here for now, but I need to talk to my daughter before I make any long-term commitments. To Lauren, too, to be fair. Thank you, Dr. Dempsey."

"Of course. Lauren, I'll see you soon, all right?" Until they knew how Lauren's zombie-ness would progress, she had to endure bi-weekly check-ups. Whether that was here or at some laboratory somewhere was yet to be determined. I worried they'd Roswell her—Mom's term for when the government made unusual monsters 'go away'—but I wouldn't bring that up. Lauren had enough to worry about already.

"Thank you, Doctor."

He left us with a friendly smile. As soon as the door closed behind him, Mom let out a long sigh of relief, double-timing it to the kitchen to grab herself a beer. "Thank Christ that's over. Congrats, Lauren. I'm not blowing smoke up your ass when I say I'm glad for you. Dr. Dempsey made the right call."

Lauren waited for Mom to come back to the living room to hug her. "Thank you, Janice. For everything." Mom patted her on the shoulder, albeit awkwardly. I think she expected Lauren to blubber and freak out, but Lauren was composed. Of course, I'd take credit for that; she was fine because I'd been supportive. I'd been supportive like a training bra. In fact, training bras were jealous of my support-like qualities.

Boo ya.

Mom gave Lauren another affectionate pat before sliding into the chair in front of her computer. "I think they're going to be cutting you some kind of stipend for expenses, too, which is nice. Dr. Dempsey will be in touch about that, though." I almost asked if that meant Lauren was on zombie welfare, but figured that wasn't very PC so I canned it. "And I'm stoked he didn't stick around all day. Nice guy and all, but now I might actually make some cash tonight. Lucky for Maggie, too. I was thinking of selling her to the creepy guy at the end of the street with the garden gnome collection." She shook the mouse to wake the computer screen, wasting no time typing in her MFer password.

"Hold on." My eyes flitted over to Lauren, then back to Mom, and I licked my lips. "There's something Lauren has to tell you. But I have to tell her first so she can tell you. Don't ask."

"What?"

"Give me five minutes." I grabbed Lauren's hand and yanked her toward the kitchen. Had Lauren chosen to stay put, I would have ripped my arm out of the socket, but as she was my new BDFF—Best Dead Female Friend—she followed along, taking a seat at the kitchen table when I asked her to. I rummaged through the junk drawer for a pen and Post-it Notes, dropping my voice to a whisper when I spoke. "Okay, you need to make sure you get this right because if you don't Mom's going to run to Boston and get sodomized by, like, four thousand angry vampires. And that'd be sad."

"Okay? I'll try."

"Awesome." I hopped up onto the kitchen counter, my bare heels kicking against the cabinet fronts. "I can't tell her what happened with Max because of the ghouling, but you can, so I need you to act as my translator. Don't include the sodomy comment. She'd get all pissy about that."

"I didn't plan on it."

"Good. So I got pulled out of the house by a vampire prince from Boston. Well, not him, but his huge bitch Russian ghoul and some mute dude named Ahmad." And the story of my Lubov-napping came to life. I'd told Mom I needed five minutes. It was evident twenty minutes later that I'd underestimated by about forever. I relayed every detail of my meeting with Max, paying particular attention to the death threats looming over Mom's head if she went aggressive. She had the right to be pissed—I was pissed about it, and I would be for a while—but she had to be careful. Pasting Max's brains all over the wall could and would go poorly. I didn't want to have to go into hiding, change my name, or drop contact with Ian because knowing me endangered him.

After thirty minutes of non-stop talking, my voice went husky, but I was pretty sure there was nothing left to say. At one point Mom poked her head into the kitchen to see what the hell we were up to, but I shooed her out before her presence choked me to death. She cast us a suspicious glare before trudging back to the living room.

"So you got it all?" I asked.

Lauren skimmed her notes and nodded. "Yeah. Geeze, Maggie. What a clusterfuck." The moment the curse came out she cringed and hunched her shoulders, like she'd committed a cardinal sin by daring to swear in my delicate presence. "Sorry! I don't... sorry."

"It's fine. You're being Janice-ized. Next thing you know your hair will be purple and you'll be singing 'Rock You like a Hurricane' in the shower. To which I'll tell you to shut up, but hey. All good."

She stood from her chair, stacking her Post-its one on top of the other. "Okay. Let me go relay. If I say anything wrong, poke me."

When we returned to the living room, I made Ta-Da arms at Mom before flinging myself onto the couch so hard, it skidded back a couple inches. She gave me one heck of a fuzzy eyeball, though whether that was because I'd abused our furniture or because I'd joined a bitch and stitch club with Lauren and she wasn't invited, I didn't know. Lauren took a deep breath, looked at me for encouragement, and then reiterated my sad, ghouly tale. As soon as Mom heard the topic, her face flushed with anger. A few times she stopped Lauren to ask questions like, "why'd he bother ghouling her" and, "so what, I'm supposed to let him *get away with taking her?*" To Lauren's credit, she gave my arguments for me, saying that though Max's methods sucked, he did give Mom a head's up that the Plasma vampire's relative was on a rampage.

Mom stared at the floor, her fingers stretching and curling over the chair armrest like a kneading cat. "He broke the law, Margaret. He broke the law and it's not okay to ignore that."

"I know," I said, because I understood exactly how she felt. We'd been bullied, and we couldn't reciprocate. We were powerless—not a feeling Mom or I were very good with. "It sucks."

"Why didn't he want you telling me?"

I motioned at Lauren, who picked through her notes to revisit my explanation. "Because he assumed you'd feel obligated to go after him, and then he'd be forced to defend himself."

"Great, so he figured he'd have to kill me. God, I hate vampires." I opened my mouth to make the oh-so-obvious comment about Jeff, but she spun and pointed a finger in my face, her eyes narrowing. I shut my mouth and smiled instead, which I think in some ways was worse. It said we both knew what I thought—*Neener neeener, you hump vampires*—but because I didn't give it voice, she couldn't bitch at me. A win-win for me.

Mom sputtered and twitched and paced for the better part of a half hour. It was clear she didn't know how to process the information. At least I was assured she wouldn't report the Plasma incident and get herself killed, which was victory one. Victory two was me figuring out how to get around Max's command.

I am such a clever monkey.

"I'm going to head up and take a shower," Mom announced, her fingers skimming her hair and flattening it to her scalp. She flicked the MF list at me so I could take a look at tonight's job listings. "There's nothing less than four stars on there, Kiddo. Sorry. 'Til the ghouling's gone we're screwed on the journeyman thing anyway. Soon, though. Jeff seems to think it'll only take a week to run its course."

"It's okay." For once, I was glad to be left behind. Lauren's ordeal had been oddly exhausting, like I'd absorbed some of her strain by osmosis. Sitting around on my butt zoning out to the boob tube sounded fantastic. Better than running around chasing rogue werewolves, anyway. That took, like, effort.

And effort sucked.

MOM LEFT FOR work at suppertime, geared up like a war machine. Lauren stared at the semi-automatic rifle strapped to her back with huge, saucer-like eyes. I reassured her that, "It's cool. She only uses that on the douchey ones. Let's get some Chinese." Lauren immediately relaxed. No better way to distract a zombie house guest than food; they were bottomless meat receptacles.

I titled our dinner Assault on Eggroll Mountain. Cartons lay scattered on the floor, looking like the broken victims of a horrific food holocaust. I had grease all over my face and duck sauce in my hair. I'd Genghis Khan'ed the *crap* out of that Chinese food, and now I was tired and bloated. Lauren, however, was totally fine, and she picked up the carnage armed with garbage bags and paper towels. I was impressed; I'd watched that chick mainline fifty pigs worth of spareribs. That she could move at all was nigh miraculous.

"Ugh. If you keep being polite and, like, helpful Janice'll kick me out and keep you. You're making me look bad."

"Sorry," she said, though I could tell by her smile she didn't mean it. I followed her out to the kitchen, so stuffed I practically waddled. We were packing the dishwasher in companionable silence when we heard the knock on the front door. I looked at the clock—half past midnight. It was way too late for it to be anyone good. For that matter, the last time someone knocked on the door it was a pair of ghouls who tried to suffocate me to death in Lubov boobies.

Lauren peered at me, then at the door. I yanked on her sleeve to keep her by my side. I won't say I was scared, but I may have been nervous that the ghouls were back. I vacillated between wanting to duck out the back door and make a run for it or heading upstairs to get a weapon from the closet. Normally it'd be a no-brainer—arm myself, shoot, ask questions later—but to get to the stairs I'd have to pass the door, and I was pretty sure Lubov could bust her way in if she wanted.

"You look like you're going to puke," Lauren said. "Are you okay?"

"If it's them, it means they know I told on Max."

"Them?"

"Ahmad and Lubov. Either Max knows or Mom didn't do the werewolf job. She went to..." I couldn't finish the sentence. Janice wouldn't have done that; she wasn't stupid enough to charge off to Boston by herself. Attempting to take on a prince, never mind a prince with live-in super ghouls, was dumb. She wasn't suicidal. Rash, yes, but not suicidal.

Whatever the scenario, the end result was something I wasn't equipped to handle. The knocking started again, this time accompanied by a loud, shouted "Hello? Maggie? Are you home?" These were not the dulcet Russian tones of a kidnapping giantess. No, this voice belonged to one Jeffrey Sampson, resident pain in my ass and fang bang extraordinaire.

Since the revelation that he sexed my mom, his name was enough to send me into a raging bitch-fit. I made the exception this time, though. I'd even go so far as to say I was *happy* to hear from him. My stomach lurched itself back into place having spent an inordinate amount of time around my knees. Gone, too, was the fear that I'd paint the kitchen walls with undigested General Gau's. Jeff wasn't my cup of tea, but he definitely wasn't Max's category of bad guy either.

I made my way to the door and opened up. Jeff stood there, pale and seemingly out of breath, one of his arms propped against the side of the house like he needed help standing. He gave me a long look, his cheek twitching and pulsing with strain.

"Get dressed. He has her."

"... what?"

"Max. He has your mother."

CHAPTER EIGHTEEN

THE FIRST QUESTION that popped into my head was 'Why does Jeff know where Mom is?' I should have assumed Mom asked him to go with her, but my gut reaction was more along the lines of 'all vampires are dicks and he works for Max and STAB STAB STABBITY STAB.' I must have telegraphed my distrust all over my face, too, because Jeff shook his head.

"Your mother asked me to act as an intermediary, but Maxim refuses to speak to her without you there. He wanted to send his ghouls, but considering what happened last time, Janice suggested I come instead. I'm not much better than they are, but... well." His shrug finished the sentence for him.

I let him stand in the doorway as I mulled that over. It was a logical explanation, yes, but he could be lying. Who knew if she was there at all? Or, if Max did have her, Jeff could have set her up in the first place. For all I knew he was Max's bestie. I could see the two of them snuggling up on the couch watching human actors on the TV the way Mom and I watched the Food Network.

Yeah, screw that. Screw him and screw vampires.

"Maggie." Lauren cleared her throat, looking between me and Jeff and back again. "If Janice is in trouble, shouldn't we go to her?"

She believed Jeff, but why wouldn't she? Calling him a monster would make her feel pretty self-conscious considering her circumstances, plus she wasn't jaded by years of Janice's 'vampires are twisted bastards' diatribes. I wished Mom had never delivered that particular spiel forty thousand times; it made having to work with her boff buddy more difficult.

"Maggie," she said again, this time clasping her hand on my shoulder to give me a squeeze. That simple touch was all I needed to get my ass in gear. I ran for the stairs. Even if this was a trap, I couldn't leave my mom in Max's clutches. Vampires weren't known for being charitable when they'd been crossed, and who knew how Mom had behaved going in. Max hadn't been kidding when he said she'd killed a lot of his kind over the last twenty years. If she'd launched a grenade at some of his folks, he'd be out for blood.

"Shit. SHIT." I stomped into my bedroom, ripping through my drawers for jeans and a sweatshirt. I strapped on some sneakers, slipped a few stakes into my waistband, and picked out my two favorite knives, wedging them into my back pockets. I headed to Mom's room to pick through her stuff when Lauren crested the top of the stairs.

"I want to go with you," she said, watching me pull a bag of water balloons out of Mom's closet. I crammed the package into the pouch on my sweatshirt before rummaging through Mom's arsenal.

"No."

"Janice has been good to me."

"You're not trained. I don't want you getting hurt."

"What's the worst they can do to me? I'm already dead. I can help."

"How?"

I grabbed two of Mom's Glocks, weighing them in my palms to see if I liked their feel, when I heard the squeal of something being dragged across the floor behind me. I turned around and stared, because *how could I not stare?* Lauren had hoisted Mom's dresser off the floor, her muscles barely flexing as she held it suspended three feet off the ground. The top of the enormous oak chest scraped across the ceiling. I knew that thing was crammed full of clothes and had to weigh at least a couple hundred pounds, yet she handled it without the slightest bit of strain.

Despite feeling sick to my stomach with worry (and, admittedly, Chinese food) I managed to find a smile. "Point made." She put it back onto the floor, adjusting the drawers that slid out during the jostling. As soon as she turned my way, I threw the bag of balloons at her. "Down on the side porch is a bunch of water jugs. Fill some of these, but not all the way. Keep 'em small. Wait, are you bad with holy water?"

She shook her head. "No. Janice tested me yesterday. It docsn't bother me."

"Good." She ran off to do as I say, her feet pounding down the steps so hard one of the pictures on the wall went off-kilter. It was an album cover autographed by all the members of Aerosmith, one of Mom's favorite bands. I fixed it, my eyes stinging at the prospect of her being in danger because of me.

"No tears. No. No." I shouldered into a holster, choosing the smaller of the Glocks and two rounds of silver-tipped ammunition. The crossbows worked better—more silver in their arrowheads—but I didn't have the same comfort level with them as I did with guns. When I tromped downstairs, Jeff stood in the living room with his arms folded across his chest. He eyed me, I eyed him, and he nodded at the couch.

"We should talk."

"Then talk," I said, though I ignored his invitation to sit down, instead adopting his militant posture.

"Fine. If I had to make a guess, he's going to use mind tricks on you and your mother to work something out regarding the Plasma situation. He's good at it. He could make you believe you're poodles if he so chose. I'm not sure if it will work on the zombie..."

"Lauren," I said. "She has a name and it's Lauren." It was convenient the times I decided to be sensitive with my labeling. But by then I itched for a fight and I didn't particularly care which vampire accommodated me. Jeff would kick my ass, of course, but getting gnawed on by his piranha fangs had to be better than the awful foreboding gurgling in my gut.

"Lauren. Yes. The point is, he could convince your mother to put one of her guns into her own mouth and pull the trigger. What do you think you'd do if he chooses to give her that command? You're his ghoul. You are blood bound to him, and you cannot betray your master. He could cut your mother in front of you and you'd be forced to watch without lifting a finger to stop it."

At some point during his speech I started shaking. And then I started heaving. I turned around to puke all over our television screen, and man, that chicken chow mein took flight. Every point Jeff made, every sentence was another kick in the craw. He was right. He was right and I knew he was right and him being right made me sick.

I couldn't handle this. I couldn't handle my *vampire master*. I was some jerk-off kid who thought she was hot shit because she had a gun. In all reality, I was in over my head. I'd let myself get ghouled because I was stupid. This was big league stuff, my mom's league, and she was in trouble. I could call Allie Silva and Tiny Tina and ask them for help, but they'd tip the feds and Max would kill my mom on principle.

"I don't know what... how..."

I felt a hand on the small of my back, tentative at first, but then it rubbed in circles. Jeff tried to comfort me. Under normal circumstances, I'd tell him to screw himself, but for the moment it was okay. It was nice to have someone feel sorry for me. Not that I wasn't doing an adequate job of pitying myself, but help was always appreciated.

"There's a way," he said quietly. "But you won't like it."

I looked at him over my shoulder, running the sleeve of my sweatshirt across my mouth. "How."

He stepped back, eyeing me like he expected me to stake him for whatever he was about to suggest. Or yuke at him. "I ghoul you and overwrite Max's tag."

"Fuck you."

"Listen to me."

"No!" Another wave of nausea made the room spin. Frantic, I looked around for something better to puke on. I liked my TV, and I didn't want it to smell bad for the rest of its existence. Under the supposition I ever got to veg out in front of it again, that is—I wouldn't be couch surfing much if a vampire ate my liver with some fava beans and a nice Chianti. "Oh, God."

"Maggie, please. Listen. It'll break Max's hold over you. He won't sense anything's awry. You were ghouled when you left, you'll return a ghoul, so he'd have no reason to be suspicious. His blood would still be in your system, too, so he'll feel you, but he won't be able to keep you in his thrall. My blood would assure immunity to his mind games."

I lunged for the paper bag our Chinese food arrived in, retching like I detoxed from some noxious drug. I didn't spew anything, but my body tried hard, sounding a lot like a backed-up garbage disposal.

Jeff tugged his blond hair out of his ponytail, shaking his head so the gold sheen fell past his ears to brush his chin. "I'm sorry. That was stupid of me to suggest. I want to help your mother. I can handle Max, but it's getting Janice out before he does something to her that worries me. If he hurts her I don't... I don't know what I'll do." The plaintive lilt to his voice stopped my heaves. I peered at him over the top of my brown paper bag. He sounded so human when he talked about my mother, like he cared about her. Like he had feelings. Like if he'd been a person I'd have said he was head over heels for her and ready to tattoo her name onto his butt.

"Do you love her?"

The question surprised me as much as it surprised him. I didn't know where it came from. Who cared if the fang loved my mom? It shouldn't make any difference. He was dead and she was not and...

Aww crap.

Him loving her made all the difference in the world. If Jeff loved Janice, he'd never hurt me intentionally, because that'd hurt her. Him offering to ghoul me was a real, honest-to-God solution to a real, honest-to-God threat. Risky, yes. Stupid on some level, oh yeah. Viable, absolutely. If everything he said was true, I'd show up tagged by Max, but Jeff's claim would mean I could act independently of the prince's command. I could shoot him or holy water him or do whatever was necessary to help my mom.

"Yes," he said, his voice soft. "Undoubtedly yes."

At least he was big enough to admit it. I wasn't thrilled he was giving my mom the cold stiff one, but knowing he cared about her meant I couldn't reject his offer as some self-serving agenda crap. Of course, it also opened up a whole slew of new questions for me, the primary one being, "How? How did this happen? She's always such a hard ass about vamps. Like, she stakes first, thinks second. How'd she get past that with you?"

He watched me stand, his eyes flicking from me to the clock on the wall and then to the door. "It's a long story."

"Sure it is, but if I'm going to take blood from you, I deserve the CliffsNotes version. I'm not getting your crazy vampire funk on me without some info, Homes."

By the confused expression on his face, I wasn't sure he understood my slang, but he explained anyway. "Three years ago, she tried to tag me for the DoPR. I was on that list of yours. I knew why she followed me, but instead of escalating it to violence, I asked her politely to leave me alone. The consideration surprised her—most of my kind would have threatened or manipulated to get their way. She was kind enough to acquiesce on the condition I help her locate a rogue vampire on her list. I agreed, we formed a partnership of sorts, and it blossomed from there. She continued to contact me when she needed help with some of her cases, and in return she let me have my freedoms. Over time, we spent time together that wasn't work related."

It wasn't a full explanation, but at least I had an idea of how their weird bang-on began. If we got out of this—no, when we got out of this—someone was sitting me down and fleshing out the rest of the ugly details. Well, not all of the details; I didn't need to know exactly when they started playing Sir Humps-A-Lot meets Lady Buck-N-Ride.

Resignation settled in my stomach like a brick. Living as a ghoul was less-than-fun with the meat-eating fetish and the sniffing and the insomnia, but what other choice was there? I wasn't a good enough ass-kicker to tackle Max. He'd already dicked me over once by kidnapping me and ghouling me without my knowledge. If there was another way for me to top him, I was clearly too dumb to figure it out. "Ugh. Fine. If you screw me over, I swear to God I'll give you a holy water enema, Jeff. Seriously. Tubes up the butt, the whole shebang."

"You're certain?"

"About the enema? Yes. The other thing, no. But I'm going to do it anyway because I'm stupid." He smiled faintly and rolled up his sleeve. I looked at his pale, bare arm and frowned, my lip curling in distaste. "Should I get a Coke for you to mix it with?"

"It's more powerful undiluted. Max is old. So it's better if it comes straight from..."

I closed the gap between us with a visible shudder. "Ugh. Shut up and gimme a hit. This is so friggin' nasty."

INEVITABLY, LAUREN WALKED into the living room at the worst possible time. I slurped on Jeff's wrist like he'd given me a cherry slushy, my lips sticky and warm with vampire blood. She paused in the doorway, her shirt pulled out from her body to hold the filled water balloons. She stared at me, stared at Jeff, and took an inadvertent step back. Somehow, we'd managed to creep out the living dead chick. That was an accomplishment somewhere.

"I can come back if you two need... erm... private time."

I glanced at Jeff to see if I'd had enough. I didn't feel trembly or quakey or any different than I had before, but he nodded at me and tugged his wrist away. Long rivulets of blood curled around his forearm, staining his arm hair and drizzling into the crease of his elbow. The gash below his palm where I'd fed mended before my eyes.

"I'll be in the washroom a moment to clean up. You may want to..." He motioned around his lips and pointed at me. I headed to the kitchen to wash the blood off my face. Drinking straight from him should have bugged me out a lot more than it did. Maybe Max's tag meant that blood had become less of a big deal. Maybe part of the magic of ghouling granted the drinker a taste for the old red.

Lauren licked her lips and shuffled her feet, clearly uncomfortable with what she'd witnessed. "A-are you okay?"

"Yeah, I'm all right."

"But you're drinking vampire blood. Would Janice be okay with that?"

If Janice was okay with me drinking alcohol until I blacked out, stabbing pixies to death with cold iron shards, and boffing my boyfriend in her house, I was pretty sure she'd be fine with this. I did what I had to do to save her. To save us. Nothing more, nothing less. Besides, I was already a ghoul. What was another couple weeks of vampire servitude? "She'll understand. Jeff's helping me out."

"By feeding you blood? Are you going to be a vampire now?"

"No. It's fine. I swear." I splashed my face one last time, using the polished steel on the front of the refrigerator to check my reflection. Blood free, I snagged a few of the balloons from Lauren's shirt, stuffing them under my sweatshirt. She watched me fidgeting and dancing around the kitchen as I socked the balloons away, slightly horrified that I manhandled my boobs.

"What are you doing?"

"Did you ever stuff your bra when you were thirteen?" I asked. I was nervous about holy water that close to my skin—the last time I'd been hit I saw Jesus—but it was a risk I had to take. They were excellent vampire repellant. At least Lauren only half-filling them meant they were harder to break.

Lauren looked more confused than she had a minute ago. "No. Well, one time. But that was with tissues because I was going to a dance."

"Then get comfortable with a couple water balloons. Best place to sock 'em away is next to the fun bags. They look natural, and give you a nice full boost." I hefted my boobs to illustrate the point. She boggled at me but did as I said, rolling her stash onto the counter and wedging two balloons into each of her bra cups. I gave her a once over, trying not to stare at her chest too long because scoping out a zombie was wrong on every single level imaginable.

"Got quadra-boob on the right, but other than that you're good."

I socked a couple more balloons into the pouch of my hoody sweatshirt. Jeff was rolling his sleeve down and buttoning it by the door when Lauren and I emerged from the kitchen. He gave me a long, assessing look. "How do you feel?"

"All right. Am I going to get different abilities than I had before? Or am I stuck with never sleeping again. It's a pretty crappy perk, if I'm being honest."

"Every vampire gives something different to their ghouls. Unfortunately we won't know what your talents are until they manifest, and that can take a bit of time. Time we don't have. I don't want Max pawing at your mother's brain." I nodded and headed outside, expecting Jeff's car to be there. Unfortunately, the driveway was empty save for Mom's truck and motorcycle. I glanced at the curb, thinking maybe he'd parked on the street again, but there was a distinct lack of vehicles.

"Uhh. How'd you get here?"

"Oh. That. I'm adept with mist. I flew here. You'll have to drive."

That'd account for why he looked so tired when I opened the front door—he'd misted his way from Boston. I rolled my eyes up to the night sky, wondering if anything would ever be easy for me. Everything I touched lately turned into a steaming crap sandwich. "I'm a minor, Jeff. I can't drive at night."

For some reason that amused him, and he flashed me two rows of glinting teeth. "Old enough to kill, not old enough to drive. How strange."

"Yeah, cute. Profound, even. You have to drive Mom's truck." I dashed back inside to get her spare keys, flinging them at his head after I locked the house. The three of us crammed into the front seat, Lauren sitting bitch between us, her elbows drawn close to her body like she feared touching either one of us for too long.

As soon as we hit the highway, something Jeff said earlier wormed its way into my thoughts. When he convinced me to let him ghoul me, he said he could "take care of Max". Max was a prince, and you didn't get to be a prince unless you were old and powerful. Weak princes were eaten alive by their own people.

"Hey, did you mean what you said about being able to handle Max? The moment he figures out you bogarted his ghoul he's gonna be pissed. And he's, like, a prince." Jeff hesitated for a moment, but then he nodded. It was clear he didn't want to get into it, but I wasn't about to let this one go. Not to be a cliché douchebag, but it was a matter of life or death. "Okay, so what, you're older?"

Another tight, curt nod.

"By how much?"

He gave me a look from the corner of his eye that wasn't all together friendly. "Enough. I am old enough."

CHAPTER NINETEEN

CONSIDERING HOW EERILY quiet the car ride was, I got to mull the 'old enough' thing all the way to Boston. Old enough for what? A vampire tricycle? Graham crackers and a glass of warm blood before his afternoon nap? Or was it the other end of the spectrum, like if he'd been made magically human he'd shrivel up into a pile of bleached bones and hair tufts? I'd seen that in an Indiana Jones movie once, where the guy went from a regular, normal dude to a withered-out husk because he drank from the false Holy Grail. Maybe before his vamping, Jeff had been the knuckle-dragging ancestor everyone referred to as the missing link. He did have a pretty prominent forehead underneath all that blond hair.

'Old enough.' What a crappy answer.

When Jeff pulled off of the highway to navigate the streets of Chinatown, I squirmed in my seat because my body felt off—all hot and tingly and wrong. Not hot like how Ian made me hot, but more like a baked potato left in the microwave too long. I'd felt nothing when I first drank Jeff's blood, but something was definitely happening then. My blood surged through my veins. My body temperature spiked, sweat oozing over my skin beneath my clothes.

Great. Mom was in trouble and all I could think about was showering to rid myself of swass—Janice's oh-so-poetic term to describe swampy, sweaty ass.

I tried to keep quiet about it, shifting and breathing heavier to cool myself off. I turned on the air conditioning in what I thought was a subtle attempt at fixing my problem, but Jeff sensed something was awry. He pulled into the parking lot of a Chinese grocery store. There were weird squid-like things hanging in the front window, and I focused on those instead of the tumultuous changes occurring inside my body. They looked like baby Cthulhus dangling from a hook.

"What's going on?" he demanded.

"Nothing."

"Tell me." I wanted to tell him to shove it out his own butt, but that whole annoying ghouling thing reared its ugly head and I was stuck doing what he said. Had I realized becoming his servant would rid me of my ability to be a jerk to him, I might have turned him down after all. What if he abused his powers and told me to clean my room and be respectful of Janice? That'd be the worst thing ever.

"I'm hot all over. Sweaty too."

"Shaking?"

I lifted my hand and my fingers trembled. Great. One drink of Jeff's blood and I was broken. "Yeah."

Jeff fished around in his pocket and handed Lauren a five dollar bill. "Go into the store and get her a bottle of water?" Lauren peered at him, then at the giant squid creatures hanging in the window. I could tell by her expression she didn't want to go in, probably because she expected them to sell her one of those monsters. I'd have made some comment about 'beware the tentacles,' but I was pretty sure that wouldn't be very helpful, plus I felt like I boiled to death inside my skin.

Lauren removed her seat belt and sighed, trudging towards the store with a sour puss. Jeff tried laying his hand against my forehead, like my Mom would when I was little, but I batted at him with a growl.

"I'm fine."

"No, you're not. Not yet anyway."

"This didn't happen when Max did his thing. What are you, a mutant vampire?"

Jeff smiled faintly, revealing the tips of his fangs. "That's because you took a lot more from me, and I'm... well. I'm older."

"About that..."

"No, Maggie." He shook his head. "I don't like talking about it, so please don't push me on this. As it stands, I'm not thrilled about dealing with Max. It draws attention to me and I've been content keeping to myself." I frowned, letting him know what I thought about his great vampire mystery. I wouldn't argue because...

I convulsed. My vision splintered in a blaze of white stars as my eyes rolled up into my head. The heat in my body became a pounding, burning pulse. I gurgled wetly, my legs kicking out as the cursed blood attacked my system. Jeff pinned my shoulders to the truck's seat, holding me down when I foamed at the mouth. It was like I'd gone full-throttle rabid raccoon. All I needed was to eat some garbage before a cop shot me and put me out of my misery.

"You'll be all right. Don't fight it and you'll be fine."

Fight it? Fight what? I didn't fight anything. I felt like molten lava ripped through my veins, that's all. *No worries here, Jeff, I was okeddy dokeddy, dickbag.* My tongue felt fat and heavy in my mouth, like a piece of wet leather. I rolled my eyes to Jeff and whimpered. He checked my temperature with the back of his hand. I probably felt slimy with sweat, like cheese left on the counter too long.

"If anything feels different, let me know. Beyond the fever."

I didn't register Lauren coming back, or the water being forced into my mouth. I remember spitting some of it in Jeff's face and finding that funny because I hadn't meant to do it, but beyond that, everything was a blur. Time passed too fast: lights streamed by, car horns honked, my heart pounded in my ears. And then, as quickly as it came, it stopped.

I looked at Jeff and then at Lauren, both of whom stared at me like I'd morphed into an alien creature. "Yo!"

"Are you all right?" Lauren asked, looking like she wanted to cry. "You turned blue for a minute."

"Yeah. I feel fine." It wasn't a lie. The burning sensation was gone, the shaking had stopped, and I could feel my temperature plummeting. I still wanted to turn on the air conditioning to arctic temperatures and blast myself in the face, but that was more because the cold helped clear my head. I needed to descramble my brains before we went toe-to-toe with a bunch of bad guys. "I'm okay. What the hell was that?"

"My magic taking root." Jeff walked around to his side of the car. He motioned for Lauren to take her position between us. When everyone was strapped in as snug as a bug, the truck eased out onto the street to head towards Max's apartment.

"Okay, so uhh. If it manifested, what can I do?"

"You don't know?"

"Know what?"

Jeff smirked. "We've had the last part of this conversation in your head."

*   *   *

So I was a psychic friend. There was some consolation to knowing if the hunting thing didn't work out, I had a backup career. 'Maggie Cunningham, Psychic to the Stars.' At least my phoneline wouldn't require me to breathe heavy or moan for money. All the power to ladies who did that, but that wasn't my deal.

I spent the better part of the next ten minutes exploring my new ability, because playing with it was infinitely less depressing than worrying about Mom. It seemed I couldn't talk to Lauren's brain, but I could definitely poke at Jeff's, to which he politely informed me that I should tap gently and *ask* to get into his head rather than barging in like a nerd kid on a Mountain Dew bender. What remained to be seen was if this was a master-to-ghoul thing, or if I could do this mind stuff with other people, too. Lauren was outside of my scope because her brain was dead. It wasn't quasi-dead like a vampire, but for reals dead, like a big pile of sludgy meat in her skull. She was amazingly cognizant for a girl who had the same brain function as a bowl of oatmeal.

"So Max'll be able to tell if I'm talking to you while we're in there, huh," I said to Jeff with my new Jedi mind trick. "None of this mental crap when we're around him?"

"He has to actively be looking for your thoughts, but if he chooses to snoop, yes. He'll hear you. He was locked on your mother earlier, so hopefully that'll continue when we arrive. I'd suggest not thinking about the ghouling, though. If he clues into it, we're in for trouble."

"... you realize telling me not to think about something means I will ten times harder."

Jeff smiled. "I know. The best I've ever been able to come up with is reciting song lyrics in my head. Over and over. It's surprisingly effective."

Song lyrics. I could do that. Row, row, row my boat until my eyeballs popped out of my skull.

We pulled into the garage at Max's building at half past one in the morning. I couldn't see much from where we parked, but then I couldn't see much the first time I was here either. Lubov had made sure to squash most attempts at area recognition by shoving my face into her chest. If I'd been into six and a half foot women with shoulders broad enough to fill a doorway and Christina Aguilera hair, I'd have been in dreamland. Sadly for Lubov, I preferred tall skinny basketball players with shyness issues. Ian's lack of blue eyeshadow was also a point in his favor.

"When we go in, let me do the talking," Jeff said, trotting down the sidewalk to get to the front doors. A man in a navy blue uniform let us in, giving a curt nod as we passed him by. Jeff didn't speak again until the elevator doors closed behind us. "No acts of aggression. Don't glare, swear, or provoke. If you do, things will escalate more than they need to. He'll know he can't control you anymore."

"Yes, Dad."

"Maggie."

For a moment, Jeff had the same warning tone Mom used, like he'd gotten an annoying, parental STD from her. It made me smirk, which in turn made Lauren smirk. No worries about us being aggressive when we got upstairs; we were too busy being smarmy peckerheads. Obnoxious had to be preferential to confrontational, though, and Jeff looked too distracted to care much anyway.

Max's apartment was the same nouveau chic douche palace I remembered, though this time instead of ocean sounds I heard wind chimes when I stepped inside. I glanced around to see if he had a set anywhere, but no, it was piped through invisible speakers again, another relaxation CD doing its thing. My eyes skipped to the couch. Janice sat there in her Red Sox ball cap and tufts of pink hair sticking out along the sides. Her lack of weapons was strange. She had on her regular hunting clothes, but her gear was stacked on the floor across the room in a useless pile. Mom never would have taken those off willingly, which meant Max was already in her head.

Fantastic.

"Maggie. So glad you joined us!" Max stood, wearing a pale gray Abercrombie tee shirt and a pair of jeans that looked new off the rack. A pair of earthy crunchy sandals exposed his perfect toenails. Ahmad moved in to Max's left, eyeballing me like a good guard dog. He'd been friendly towards me during the kidnapping, but that seemed to be over now. Max tutted at him and shook his head. "She's family now. Stop that." Ahmad scowled. He wasn't buying that family crap any more than I was.

Max gave me an assessing look, and I realized it was time to break out the song trick. All my row-your-boat intentions flew out the window; for some horrible reason, the only song I could think of was the Sex Pistols "Friggin' in the Riggin'"— possibly the crudest song in the history of rock and roll. Mom played the crap out of their tapes for a while, and to this day I can recite most of their discography from memory. Other kids got lullabies. I got "Anarchy in the UK."

Max, picking up on the rampant cussing in the Sea Chanty From Hell, stared at me incredulously. I gave him a weak, gassy smile, forcing my brain through the next stanza, bouncing with every mentally-screeched swear word. He cleared his throat and looked past me, probably thinking I was as soft as a sneaker full of baby crap. It was for the best; the lyrics only got worse after that.

"Lubov, get them drinks. And... who is this?" Max motioned at Lauren. "One of Maggie's friends?"

"She's my charge." Mom turned toward us. I smiled at her, and she returned it, but it was stiff, her cheek twitching like she'd gnawed on electrical wires. "She's in the DoPR's protective care. Her name's Lauren."

"Sit *down*, Janice," Max said. I could hear the weight to his words. Mom could, too, and she plunked herself onto the couch because she had no other choice. I did, though, and I crossed the room to stand behind her, putting my fingers on her shoulder. She grabbed my wrist and squeezed. Lauren came to stand beside me, and the three of us peered at Max like an angry cluster of estrogen.

Lubov returned bearing cans of Coke on a platter, putting them onto the table in front of Mom. When she stood, she cast me a huge smile, like she was legitimately glad to see me. Too bad she was one of Max's people—she'd have been a likable person otherwise. I hoped I didn't have to shoot her later.

"Maggie, it is good to be seeing you again."

"Hi, Lubov."

"Are you thirsty?"

"No, thanks." I didn't add the part about "I'd rather drink donkey piss than anything you guys give me" because it went without saying. Max had to know I wasn't happy about the ghouling. Putting a Coke in front of me as a stark reminder of how he'd tricked stupid Maggie Cunningham felt a lot like an unspoken "Fuck you."

The more I thought about it, the more I wanted to tell him to shove it. So many scathing things twisted around my tongue, threatening to burst from my mouth like explosive diarrhea, but a gentle brain poke from Jeff kept my temper in check.

Don't.

I heard him clear as day, like he'd said the word to my face instead of piping it into my noggin. Fine. He was right. Letting Max know I thought he was a douche wouldn't do a whole lot other than give me away. I might feel better for five minutes, but at what cost? I shifted my weight from one foot to the other, casting my eyes to the floor.

"I'd like to get up now," my mom said.

"No. Not until we've had a talk."

"This is considered a magical attack by forcing me to do something against my will. Under clause six one b, chapter twelve, you can't..."

"I'm not talking to you, but to your daughter. In fact, you stop talking altogether," Max snapped. Mom shut up because she had to. I felt her stiffen under my hand, her body trembling. She was furious, and now she couldn't give voice to it. She couldn't explain to Max which laws he broke. The offenses against me were now piled on top of offenses against her. Jeff said Max would tinker with Mom's head, so he probably figured he'd be able to erase all of this and clean slate her before he was through.

Again I wondered how Mom broached the subject; had she pointed a gun and told Max to drop? Had she mooned him? Had she told him his mother smelled of elderberries?

"You need to stop, Max," Jeff said, his voice quiet. "The less free will you allow her, the worse this will go."

Max sniffed and threw himself into a chair, leaning back until his chin rested on his chest. He peered at Mom, then at me, his fingers clasped together on top of his sternum. "How did this happen, Maggie? I told you not to tell her. I explicitly said..."

"Not to tell a living soul," I said. "I didn't. I told an unliving soul." He clearly had no idea what I talked about, and I jerked my thumb at Lauren. "She's the living dead and I told her."

He peered at Lauren, suddenly a lot more interested in her. He crooked a finger to motion her near, but she stayed put, wedging herself into my side. She was scared, but then, she hadn't been exposed to monster shenanigans when she'd been alive so this was a whole new experience. I should have warned her it wouldn't be fun. She'd insisted on coming along to help, though, and I doubted she'd have taken no for an answer if the whole bureau-lifting thing was any indication.

"No, thank you."

Her politeness made Max smile, and he sat up straighter in his chair. "How sweet! Come here, dear." Again he added that weight to his words, like he'd done to me, like he'd been doing to Mom since we'd arrived. And yet...

Lauren stayed put.

"No, thank you. I'm comfortable where I am."

She was immune—no brain waves meant he couldn't razzle-dazzle his way into Lauren's thoughts. True fact: our zombie was totally kick-ass awesome, and he could suck it for trying to mind-molest her.

Max didn't see it that way, of course, and he went back to his new old staple, the glower. "Are all the women in your household difficult?"

"Uhh, yeah, but in our defense you kidnapped me and now you're holding my mom hostage. That's bound to annoy us."

"I took you to *help* you. To *save* you from Matthew. And your mother came to me. I didn't take her from anywhere."

"Bollocks," Jeff said. He closed the distance between himself and Max, not stopping until he could jam his finger in Max's face. "You helped *yourself*. You didn't want Matthew coming after you for his descendant's death. Instead of properly watching your fledgling, you shoved her off onto a handler, and that handler made a grievous error, which I'm sure he died for. Far easier to punish him than yourself for being an irresponsible sire." Jeff glanced at me and Mom. "I hadn't thought of this before, but I'm going to venture a guess Matthew wouldn't want monetary restitution, he'd want blood. Lizzie was their peace treaty, assurance that the two territories would play nicely for the next twenty years, and Maxim cocked it up. The DoPR report would have outed him, so he thought to scare you away from filing it."

I'd never heard the term 'cocked it up' before; we said screwed up or fucked up or messed up, but not cocked up. I liked it, it had a ring to it, but it was an unusual turn of phrase, and I socked it away for later usage. Anything to add to my vast and varied dictionary of obscenities was okay in my book.

Maxim rose from his chair, face angled in such a way that no matter how he looked at us, it was down his nose. Douchebag. "Do you know how dangerous these accusations are?"

Jeff eased toward my mother, never giving Max his back. "Of course I do. But I have to wonder if Matthew would be so stupid as to put a bounty on a hunter's head? Another monster, perhaps, but the moment he discovered Lizzie attacked Janice he'd have to let it go. Retaliation against an agent of the federal government would result in a purge of his domain. The only alternative he'd have is to come after *you*. But Maggie doesn't know our politics. You used the child's ignorance against her, didn't you? That's low, Maxim."

I disliked being called a child. I loathed being called ignorant, even if it was the right word to use. But how could I have known any better? I was targeted. I was the stupid apprentice versus my Mom's two decades of hunting experience. Maxim used that to his advantage to save his own ass.

What a dick.

Max curled his lip at Jeff, his brown eyes somehow managing to appear cold. "Do you forget your place? Do you know who you're talking to?"

Jeff smiled, revealing every one of his razor sharp teeth. He fussed with the cuffs of his shirt sleeve, unbuttoning them and rolling them up to his elbows. "I'd ask you the very same thing, Maxim. Do you know who you're talking to? Because I am guessing you don't."

CHAPTER TWENTY

MALE VAMPIRE POSTURING was a lot like male human posturing; there was a lingering stare that could be mistaken for sexual tension in another scenario. Also present was the metaphorical prick waving. It got so bad, I fully expected Max and Jeff to whip out their schlongs and beat each other with them. Maybe when they clashed, there'd be that humming sound of colliding light sabers. I'd have to close my eyes through it because seeing Mom's boyfriend's penis once was accidental, twice was perverted, but at least I'd be able to hear them thanks to the *Star Wars* sound effects.

"I have zero reason to let them go," Max said.

"You have every reason to let them go." Jeff leaned in, close enough to Max's ear he could kiss it if he wanted (and wouldn't that add another level of weird to an already weird evening) and whispered beneath his breath. I wasn't good at lip-reading, so I had no clue what was going on. No one else did either. Mom leaned forward like she might be able to overhear if she got close enough. Lauren cocked her head to the side like a confused cocker spaniel. Lubov peered, and Ahmad... Ahmad went tenser, if that was possible. He was already a twitchy, rigid mess—a cobra raising its hood to strike.

Max recoiled from Jeff like he'd been slapped. I was now triply curious about Jeffrey Sampson; what horrible secret did he have that could make a city leader flinch? Was he that old? Was he that powerful? Was he vampire Gestapo? I had so many questions, but I didn't ask any of them. I was too busy watching Max retreating. His unease fueled his ghouls' unease. Lubov stood straighter, moving to stand by her master's elbow, and Ahmad crouched, poised like a cat before it leapt onto a counter. Max put his hand on his lover's shoulder and squeezed, warning him away from doing something stupid.

"No. No, don't. It's not worth it. *He's* not worth it." Max sneered and turned to Mom, his expression suggesting that if he had the opportunity to wear her kidneys as earrings, he'd do it. "Get out of my sight and stay away from my people. You're free to do as you will. Maggie and I, however, need to *talk*."

The moment his thrall broke on Mom she was up and off the couch, crossing the room to retrieve her stuff. I watched her reassemble her gear, layering it in such a way that she could move freely if push came to shove. The gun went over her shoulder, the stakes were wedged into their holders on her belt. At least four knives disappeared inside her boots and pockets. "I can't and won't leave you alone, and you're staying away from my kid. I'm calling you in for kidnapping, forced ghouling, and two counts of magical attack, so get yourself a lawyer. You're lucky I don't call a scrub squad to wipe your ass off the planet, fathead."

Max didn't look appreciative. In fact, he looked furious, but that was the least of our troubles. Mom turned toward us, and as she moved the gun on her shoulder shifted, sliding down a few inches as its weight rebalanced. The barrel swung with it. Ahmad must have assumed that Mom went aggressive, because he became a blur of speed, lunging for her. He'd been wound up tighter than a bull's ass at fly time since I got there, so I should have seen something like this coming, only I didn't.

Before anyone could do a damned thing about it, my mother was lifted off her feet and thrown across the room. *Slam*! Her back hit the wall with a wet snap. She went slack, her eyes rolling up into her head. She reminded me of a broken dandelion with a straight stem and a lolling flower. Her body slid to the floor, her legs akimbo, her arms leaden by her side. Her gun was the only thing keeping her from lying flat; it propped her at an odd angle, like she rested on her elbow.

Looking at her limp form, I convinced myself Ahmad had killed her. And now he stood over her body, staring down at her like he was shocked by what he'd done. I shook from head to toe, wanting to cry and scream and hurt things. I wanted to beat him to death with my fists, to claw his eyes out for hurting the one person who loved me no matter what stupid thing I'd done. I didn't, though, because Janice Rule Number One came screaming into my brain: when a monster shows aggression, you shoot and worry about everything else later. Monsters were faster and stronger, the only thing we had on them was the element of surprise.

If that was the case, this would surprise the crap out of everyone. I pulled the Glock and switched off the safety. Max screeched from somewhere behind me, panicking that I was about to cap his boyfriend. It changed nothing. I pulled the trigger. Once, twice, three times. The shots took the ghoul between the shoulder blades. The blasts made me flinch, my ears ringing at the deafening explosions in the small confines of the apartment, but I didn't care. I watched the red blossoms appear on the back of Ahmad's shirt, blood saturating the thick cotton before he staggered and dropped to his knees. He turned his head to look at Max with a wet gurgle, and for a moment I thought he'd say something.

I wasn't down with that. I put a fourth bullet in the back of his skull, watching brain matter and bits of skull fly, some of it painting the floor, the wall, and my mother's prone body. He fell onto his face with a thud. It was the first time I'd played executioner; whenever we'd done jobs in the past Mom was the one who pulled the trigger. That had all changed, and I didn't feel anything. I was empty, a void. I'd killed someone and I didn't give a damn. What did that say about me?

I ran through the room to get to my mother. I wanted to get Ahmad away from her, to drag her out of this place and call the police. To clean the splotches of blood off her face because it made me feel faint to look at them. None of it was possible with a vampire latched to my back. Max leapt on me, riding me like a bad pony. His fangs ripped through my shirt and ravaged my shoulder. I whipped around, lurching my way toward the couch so I'd have something to cling to. Max was lean, but he was a hundred and sixty pounds of lean, and I wasn't used to lugging that around.

I used the butt of the gun to strike him in the face. A fang grazed the back of my hand, slicing open my knuckles as effectively as a razor blade. He growled and struck again, this time at my forearm, tearing a quarter-sized piece of flesh from the fat near my elbow. He snorted as he swallowed it whole, sounding more animal-like than human, and I screamed.

"SOME HELP HERE, JEFF!"

"Working on it," he growled, closer than expected. "Get to your mother." Max was torn off my back, but he did not go gently. His claws raked my chest and arms, flaying my skin wide. I erupted with fresh shrieks. My upper half felt like I'd been inserted head-first into a blender. I bled from my right shoulder and arms. I throbbed and hurt in ways I'd never imagined possible. The holy water dousing hadn't been this bad. But it didn't matter. None of it mattered. I was alive, but my mother...

I had to get to Mom. I had to see if I could help her.

I stumbled across the room, light-headed and woozy. I stepped over Ahmad's legs, about to kneel beside Mom, when Lubov charged me from across the room. She was the bull, I was the red flag, and we were going to dance this dance. I knew she had to come after me on basic principle, but there was something sad about it, too. I wanted to like her, and this was definitely going to put us at odds. I mean, if she got her hands on me she'd pull me into so many pieces I'd resemble bloody Tinkertoys. There was no way you could be friends after something like that. Ripping out someone's spleen was an anti-friendship activity.

I lifted the gun to fire, aiming for a shoulder instead of a kill-shot, but my arm shook so much, I could barely keep my grip. Before I could humiliate myself by shooting wide (or worse, not at all) Lauren stepped in front of me, braced her legs, and became a zombie wall, protecting me from the battering ram of a Russian headed my way. Between Lubov's size and super-strength, skinny little Lauren should have been thrown halfway across the universe upon impact. A normal person would have become a human lawn dart, sailing through the glass windows and splattering on the concrete forty-four floors below. The good news for me and everyone else was Lauren had her own freaky-weird strength thing. She dug her feet into the carpet and shoved back. It was *Clash of the Titans*, except in this case Titan One was an undead girl who murdered ducks and Titan Two was a giantess with a propensity for tit smother.

They locked arms, shoving at one another. Back and forth, back and forth. Lauren managed to shove Lubov back a few feet, but Lubov was not to be outdone. She picked up an end table and chucked it because, you know, that's what end tables are for when you're seven feet tall and have nothing better to do. Lauren punched it to splinters. I wish that was an exaggeration, but the girl's hand made contact with it and it exploded, sending pieces flying everywhere. I covered my face to avoid being impaled by shrapnel.

Lubov eyed her adversary before lifting Max's fine leather couch. I had visions of her swinging it around like an enormous baseball bat, pummeling me and Janice with it until we were paste smears on the carpet. It wasn't a happy thought, so I scampered over to my mom, looping my hands under her arms and pulling her across the floor toward the fountain in the foyer. She never stirred or made a sound. I whimpered aloud, wishing more than anything that she'd sit up and bitch at me for screwing up a monster job. But she didn't.

I tugged off my sweatshirt so I could tuck it under Mom's head. Every brush of fabric against my wounds made me yelp, and lifting my arms was utter agony, but I persevered, ignoring the fact that I stood around in a sports bra loaded with holy water balloons. I wadded the sweatshirt into a ball and slid it under Mom's neck, my fingers hovering above the base of her throat. I didn't want to touch her, afraid that I'd feel nothing, but I couldn't avoid it forever.

I swallowed my fear and pressed my fingers to her pulse, my eyes drifting to her chest to determine if she breathed. I nearly squealed when I felt the faint beat beneath my fingertips. She was alive. Screwed up and completely out of commission? Yes. But she was alive, and maybe if we got the hell out of here she'd stay that way.

I was intent on getting her to safety so I could safely call an ambulance, but another fiendish shriek stopped me. I thought maybe one of the girls had hit the other with a bookshelf, but it was the vampires. Jeff had his arms looped under Max's, holding him in a full nelson. Max banshee-wailed, his teeth gnashing, his feet skidding over the carpet. His eyes were red-rimmed and frenzied, a lot like Lizzie had been back at Plasma before she'd dragged me through the van window. It was that sub-human blood lust I thought they reserved for virgin snacking. Apparently, they could channel it at people they hated, too.

Lucky me.

Jeff's brow was furrowed, his body plastered with sweat. He had to concentrate to keep the vampire in his grasp from chasing after me. I glanced back at Mom's body. For all that I wanted to get her to safety, I couldn't abandon Jeff and Lauren. God forbid something happened to one of them after I left. Sure, Mom was the most important person in the world to me, but these people had helped her, too. They'd come to keep her safe. They weren't cannon fodder to help Maggie's cause.

They were my bitches and I had my bitches' backs.

I jerked a holy water balloon out of my bra, exposing a good chunk of boob in the process, but oh well. A little Maggie nudity never killed anyone. Ian survived it anyway, so I took that as proof that I didn't turn people to stone like mini-Medusa. I pinched the top of the balloon closed and used a pocket knife to puncture the tie, oh-so-carefully holding it aloft. I didn't want it to squirt on me, but I was willing to take the chance. It might be battery acid to a ghoul, but to a vampire, it was molten lava.

Approaching a frothing vampire intent on taking fleshy chunks from your person was a gut check, but I squashed the instinct to flee by telling myself this was what hunters did. They pushed their fears aside and got the job done, for better or worse. I lifted the balloon and gave it a hard squeeze, propelling the holy water at Max's chest, doing my best to avoid Jeff's arms where they touched. The moment it made contact with Max's skin, there was a burning smell, like a hamburger left on the grill too long. Max screamed, his spine bowing into such a pronounced C I thought he'd snap in half. Jeff braced his legs further apart to compensate for Max's thrashing. I pulled a stake from my waistband. I felt dizzy and sick, but I had to persevere. I had to finish it so me, Mom, Jeff, and Lauren could go home. Or to the hospital. Whatever.

Any place was better than this place.

"Do it," Jeff said. My eyes snapped to Max. He screeched in my face, roaring like a lion with its foot stuck in a trap. Despite the ruckus, I could hear the holy water eating through his skin, crackling and snapping like a bowl of Rice Krispies as it melted his flesh to pudding. For a single moment I told myself maybe it was enough, he'd learned his lesson and he could go back to doing Pilates and listening to tidal sounds and birds chirping in trees, but then he hucked a huge, bloody loogie at me, gobbing up my right cheek. Any compunction I had about killing him went right out the window. Ghouling me, lying to me, hurting my mom, and now spitting on me—it was enough.

I'd had enough. Fuck him and fuck the horse he rode in on.

It hurt like hell to raise my torn, ragged arms over my head, but I brought the stake down all the same. It struck him in the sternum, making him howl as the tip raked over bone. I did it again, the second time jabbing him in the soggy, ruined cavity of his chest. Another scream. On the third go I paused, taking a deep breath to clear my head before aiming up under his rib cage on the left side. Janice had shown me how to heart strike on ballistics dummies before; I knew how to take a vampire out with one clean strike. And take him out it did. The moment the stake pierced his heart, Max's eyes bulged, his body going rigid before he deflated like a man-sized balloon.

I could have done the heart strike the first time and ended it all in one go, but the fact was he'd made me angry and I wanted to hurt him. Petty, yes, but who cared. The important thing here was that Maxim, the prince of Boston, was dead and I, Maggie Cunningham, had killed him.

And I killed him good.

CHAPTER TWENTY-ONE

MAX'S BODY FELL to the floor with a meaty thwack. Staking him was not the great fix-it you'd expect. There were sucky things left to handle, namely Mom's health. She was out like a light, and I knew enough about concussions to say if she was unconscious this long, it could mean major brain bleeding. That would result in a case of the dead if we didn't get her to the hospital. Of course, it might not be a concussion at all, but by the way her head hit the wall, I wouldn't rule it out.

I was about to tell Jeff to call an ambulance, but he was too busy looking across the room to pay me any mind. I followed his gaze. Sometime during Max's staking, Lauren had gotten the upper hand on Lubov, and was presently straddling her on the floor with one hand on her neck, the other pinning her arms to her chest. Lubov didn't struggle. Considering the lady swung couches around like Superwoman on crack not two minutes ago, it was hard to believe she'd give up like that.

"What's going on?"

"She lost her power when Max died," Jeff said, crouching beside her. "She has no strength." He dismissed Lauren with a flick of his wrist, offering Lubov a blood-smeared hand.

She ignored it and climbed to her knees, attention focused on the decimated body of her former master. She let out a low whimper and rubbed her eyes with her fists, looking like an over-tired three-year-old who didn't want to go to bed. A monstrously huge three-year-old who didn't want to go to bed, but still.

"We have a problem." Jeff spoke directly to my mind again. I scratched at my head like that'd exorcise his voice but it didn't help. For all that having a telepathic connection to someone was cool, I could now see his point about it being invasive. He hadn't tapped gently to come into my head; he'd barged in, grabbed himself a beer, and settled onto Maggie's brain couch. He was a squatter taking up space that wasn't his. Sure, I'd done it to him earlier, but that was me and thus okay.

Hypocritical? You bet.

"Yeah, like Mom. We need to get her to a doctor."

"And you should have your shoulder looked at, but first what do we do about Lubov? I have my opinions, but I don't want to further upset you. I think I'm going to have to—" His shoulders sagged. For all that he was a mother-humping bloodsucker with a propensity for hoarding secrets, he seemed like he earnestly didn't want to kill my Russian nemesis. Okay, Lubov wasn't my nemesis, but calling her that made me feel like a total bad-ass. James Bond had at least three Russian nemeses, and Rocky and Bullwinkle had Natasha and Boris. That was some elite company right there.

"—she was loyal to him, and if she talks about this to his other followers, it will make more trouble for all of us," Jeff finished.

"No," I said, though I must have said it aloud because Lauren jerked her eyes to me.

"'No' what?"

"Nothing. Dial 911 and get an ambulance here, please?" I flung my burner phone at her and it whacked her on the boob. Obscene strength, yes. Catlike reflexes, no. She walked to the foyer with the phone attached to her ear, pawing through Max's mail to find his address.

Lubov lifted her face to me. Blue makeup smeared her temples, and there were tracks of mascara under her eyes making her look like a hosed-down clown. It was the most pathetic thing I'd seen in a long time.

"Mental, Margaret. This is between you and I."

"Oh, don't you start. It's Maggie. For Christ's sake. If you call me Margaret again I will punch you in the nuts, Jeff. I swear."

"Maggie. Fine. Focus, please."

"Focus this. Anyway, don't kill her. She was nice to me during Max's crap and she didn't have to be. Can't you ghoul her?" He looked at me like I'd suggested he bleach his butt crack, but that didn't deter me from pleading my case anyway. "She'll be forced into loyalty and you're not stupid enough to leave a loophole if you tell her to keep quiet. She knows all the rules of ghouling, too. That's gotta be a better alternative than sending her to the Big Kremlin in the Sky."

"I won't make that choice for her. I won't force it on people."

"So ask her if she's down with it so we can get out of here and help Mom," I said aloud, making Jeff's frown deepen. I peered at Lubov, trying to ignore the fact that she appeared to be melting. If it disintegrated any further, she'd give the Wicked Witch a run for her money. "Lubov, if Jeff lets you go, you're a big pain in the ass for us. You've got a few options, but I'll be honest, they all suck. I can call the DoPR on you and you'll be taken into custody pending trial. We can kill you, which seems pretty crappy, or Jeff can ghoul you. I'd lean towards the last one. At least you and I would be the Olsen twins of creepy vampire slavery."

Jeff snorted. "Margar... Maggie. You're not my slave."

"*Focus*, Jeff," I said, using his words. Because I'm a dildo like that. "What do you say, Lubov?"

She looked from me to Jeff and then to Max's body, her eyes pinchy at the edges like she wanted to bawl. "I served *bratishka* for many years. He made mistakes, yes, but he did good things, too. He took me from a bad home. For this, I honor him." She bumped the side of her fist against her heart and bowed her head. On one hand it was cool that she did the respect thing—maybe this was her version of pouring a forty out for a lost homey—but on the other hand I wanted her to hurry up so we could concentrate on Mom. I heard Lauren talking to a dispatcher, so I knew the ambulance was en route.

Jeff didn't seem too keen on wasting any more time either. "What do you want to do, Lubov?"

It took her a moment to find her feet, but when she managed, she made her way to Jeff, dropping to a single knee before him. Her hand went to her heart like she made a most solemn vow. "I know only to serve. I will do as you say." There was a formality to her words that made me feel like my ghouling had been ghetto. She did this up with pomp and circumstance, like there was pride in the promised bond. I'd been more of a 'do you want fries with that' kinda occasion, but then, I think I was more of a drive-through ghouling girl anyway.

Jeff didn't appear to care one way or the other. He rolled up his other sleeve— the arm I hadn't gnawed on hours ago—and I left them to it, making my way to Mom to check her vitals. The pulse was stronger, and her breathing was less shallow, which had to be good. Lauren hung up the call and huddled in beside me.

"Is he... what's he going to do with Lubov?" she asked.

"Ghoul her."

"Oh. Like the blood sucking thing at the house?"

"Yep."

"Ick."

I sank to my butt to stroke Mom's pink hair, accidentally brushing off her ball cap. I wedged it onto my head, my eyes flicking to the elevator every few seconds like I could make the EMTs arrive faster by will alone.

"Your shoulder's all bloody," Lauren said, her voice quiet. "Are you okay?"

"I'll be all right," I said, giving her a dry, humorless smile. "And thanks for everything. You've been awesome."

"It's nothing."

"It's everything. You rock."

"Thanks, Maggie. I'm glad I could help."

OUR MERRY BAND of freaks got Mom to the hospital at two in the morning. I rode in the ambulance with her, Jeff drove everyone else in the truck. Up to that point, I'd been so amped on adrenaline I hadn't processed the hideous crap we'd been through, nor had I acknowledged the pain wracking my body. Watching the doctors swing shut behind Mom's gurney shattered that. I promptly ran to the bathroom to lose my shit. I'd have to get my injuries attended to, but not yet. Not until I felt like I could stand in front of a doctor without blasting weepy snoogers at him.

I specifically chose the single stall handicapped bathroom so I could have the room to myself while I sniveled. And snivel I did, burying my face into my bicep and letting every ounce of angst come pouring out. Gurgling whines, snotty nose, bulging, red-rimmed eyes—I had it all. Lauren knocked on the door at one point to make sure I wasn't trying to hang myself with toilet paper and I assured her I was okay, but I wasn't. Not only was my mom in some serious danger, I'd killed two people tonight. I'd ended lives. Bad lives, yes, though Max was easier on my conscience than Ahmad. Ahmad had protected his boyfriend. If someone had threatened Ian, would I have been able to stand by with my thumb up my butt? Or would I attack, too? Of course, Ian wasn't a villainous scumbag vampire dickhole, so maybe Ahmad should have chosen better company.

Justification. I needed to justify those four bullets I put into that ghoul and I couldn't do it alone.

I dialed. I knew I shouldn't have—it was the middle of the night—but I called Ian because I wanted to hear that I wasn't a bad person, that I'd done the right thing and that I wouldn't become Satan's footstool when I died. I wasn't exactly a religious person per se, but I believed something happened in the great hereafter involving judgment. I'd seen how magic worked in our world, how karmic balance tended to play out when left to its own devices, and I had to believe some of that magic existed when we went tits up to our final maker. I didn't want to burn in Hell. I would for being a foul-mouthed, slutty, well-meaning murderess, but I didn't want to.

Ian picked up the phone with a raspy, sleep-ridden voice. I was so glad to hear him, I cried louder, likely blasting my Maggie-wails right into his ear. I could hear him saying my name over and over, but I wasn't capable of answering. Actual conversation was so beyond me, it was like I'd regressed to being eight months old. If I myself again, it was all over.

"Mags, what's up? Hey, hey, babe. C'mon. You're worrying me. 'Sup?"

"M-Mom got hurt," I managed.

"Oh, man. She okay?"

"D-don't know. Sorry to call so late. I... I..." I stammered 'I' thirty more times and took a deep breath, trying to regain my composure. "She hit her head and they're trying to see if her brain's bleeding or whatever."

He took a long, deep breath, then promptly exhaled it right into the receiver of the phone. It hurt my ear, but I wouldn't complain. "Do you want me to come? I can. I gotta ask my 'rents about the car, but..."

"No. I'll be okay. There's no point 'til I know more. I wanted to talk to you." That made me sound so lame, but at least I wasn't professing my love or writing my initials next to his in a heart on the bathroom stall wall. I had my dignity. Sort of. "Sorry I woke you."

"It's okay. That's... man, that sucks so bad."

"I know. And I killed someone tonight. Two people." I had to hope my less-than-graceful announcement didn't go over like a fart in a spacesuit. I kept thinking aspects of my strange lifestyle would be the straw that broke the camel's back and Ian would run from me, but so far he'd hung in there like a champ. What were one or two deaths on top of my laundry-list of my other bizarro quirks? "A vampire and his ghoul. I feel weird about it."

I told him the rest of the story, talking about how Ahmad hurt Mom, and how Max hurt me because of it. While I talked, I flicked flakes of dried blood off of the back of my hand. Whether it was mine or Max's, I didn't know. The nurses and doctors had taken a look at me and Jeff when we walked into the emergency room and assumed I was in danger. They'd tried to cart me out back, but I showed them my hunting credentials and assured them that my mom was the patient, that the blood on me belonged to a dead vampire. Of course, I'd lied, and now that everything shifted back into focus, I realized I had to get off the phone and get myself stitched. I felt woozy.

"Anyway," I said, wrapping up my explanation. "I don't know how to feel about it." It was too much to hope that Ian would exonerate me, and as the silence stretched between us, I worried that once again I'd gone one step too far.

Then he spoke.

"He hurt your mom. He could have killed you both. You survived. I'm sorry you feel like crap, but you did good. Well. Whatever. You saved everyone. I'm glad you're okay."

It was the right thing to say. My self-doubts faded, relief and pride taking their place. Ian was right; I'd only done what I had to do. I may have saved everyone. Of course, this led to the train of thought that I was so much more amazing than I had given myself credit for. People should thank me for the privilege of standing in the room with me and breathing my air. I deserved a medal for my overly-inflated chest.

"Thank you, Ian," I said. "I needed to hear that. Like, you have no idea. Thanks."

"No sweat. Hey, call me when you hear something, yeah? And good luck. Take care of yourself. Hope Janice is okay."

"Yeah, I will. G'night."

"G'night."

I hung up the phone, pushed myself to standing, and headed for the nurse's station.

TEN HOURS, TWENTY-three butterfly stitches, and a nap in a very uncomfortable chair later, we had Janice's diagnosis. She had a hairline fracture in an upper vertebrae. It wasn't enough to be considered a broken neck, but it was enough to cause her so much pain her body shut down. Somehow, luck be praised, she'd avoided a massive concussion.

Jeff, Lauren, Lubov, and I slumped into each other's sides as we waited for Mom to wake from her ordeal. I was tired, but the posture was more a result of boredom than anything else; hours of late late late shows would make anyone's eyes bleed. I figured Jeff would take off when the sun came up, but he stuck around, asking all of the important adult questions I didn't think of when the doctors came by, like "will she need physical therapy" and "how long will she be impaired?" The doctor's answer to both was "I don't know yet." It was clear by the lack of forthcoming information we'd be sitting and waiting awhile. Who knew how long Mom's stay would be.

By noon, pins and needles stabbed my butt, making me feel like I'd sat on a porcupine. I got up to pace, glancing at Jeff every few seconds. He seemed deep in thought, worry lines appearing on his brow when he thought no one looked. I would have asked him what he stressed about, but I figured he'd be Mister Enigma about that, too, so I went another direction with my questions.

"So if you could get Mom out of there with a whisper to Max, why didn't you? Why'd you come get me? Seems like a lot of extra work."

Lubov stiffened at Max's name, but Jeff put a hand on her knee to reassure her. I don't know if he blasted her with magical vampire juju or what, but she relaxed and went back to thumbing through her *Glamour* magazine. Maybe she'd pick up a new makeup tip that wasn't 'Roll your face on the Revlon counter and see what happens.'

"He wouldn't listen to me without you there. He knew you couldn't lie to him as his ghoul. I think he wanted you to confirm or deny my claims." He hesitated before adding, "I was also afraid it'd get violent, and though I knew I could handle Max on his own, his entourage... well. I needed more assurances that Janice would get out alive."

"So you called in Team Bad Ass." I grinned at Lauren to let her know she was part of Team Bad Ass, but she had no reply. Lounging in an uncomfortable hospital chair all night long was hard on the undead, too.

"I used all of my resources. Take that as you will." He cast me a wan smile that revealed no fang, and I returned it before my stomach let out a hunger gurgle that sounded like Swamp Thing's mating call. Apparently, with Max's hold broken thanks to his deadification, my whole bionic-woman-never-needing-to-eat thing was over. At that moment, I'd have skinned a cat alive for a bagel and cream cheese.

"I'm totally starving. I'm gonna hit Dunkin' Donuts for some chow. Lauren, you want a sausage thinger? Or..."

I didn't finish the thought because the doctor burst through the double hospital doors. At first he had no expression, but the moment he neared us his whole face lit up. Something was good. Something had made him happy. I picked up my stomach from the floor and took a deep breath.

"She's awake," he said. "And she's asking for all of you."

CHAPTER TWENTY-TWO

THEY WEREN'T GOING to let Mom out for a while, and though I loved her a lot and was more than willing to visit during the day, I went home with Jeff the next morning. I had my reasons for wanting to go, the first of which was getting Lauren to a place where she could comfortably scarf dead animals without the temptation of human brains everywhere. The girl was plenty nice, but starve her too long and who knew what would happen? She'd either go on a person bender or raid McDonald's for their pretend cow patties. I wasn't risking it.

There was also Ian to consider. I wanted to see him. I'd texted him after we got Mom's prognosis and told him I'd be home the next day so maybe we could get together. He sent me a smiley face and heart emoticons in return, and it made me grin like an idiot. I was so smitten with my new boyfriend that I acted all gag-worthy and lame. Mom knew it, too. When I told her why I was going home, she grinned at me from her hospital bed and said, "Aww, Margaret Jane has a boyfriend. How cute!"

I let her get away with her smart mouth because she was all broken and crap, but next time, she'd get a karate chop to the lady junk.

I kissed her on the forehead and packed my stuff to go. Lubov stayed in the hospital's waiting room while Jeff drove us, mostly because she wouldn't fit in the truck. The trials of being a giantess, I guess. She waved to me as we left, a smile on her mouth. At some point she'd taken the time to reapply her battle paints, and I couldn't help but think her lipstick shade was called Retina Stab.

"I will be seeing you soon, Maggie. You are good girl."

"Uh huh. Bye, Lubov. Take care of yourself."

The drive back to the house was relatively quiet because we were all exhausted. When we pulled into the driveway, Lauren hopped out of the truck, but I paused to eye my new vampire overlord. I hadn't considered Jeff my master because my brain had already slotted him into the category of 'half-dead dude boning my mom.' The reality was he could control me if he wanted to, and because I was smarter than the average bear, I knew I should keep a quasi-copacetic relationship with him until his tag wore off.

Otherwise, he could make me clean toilets with a toothbrush. Not cool.

"So, uhh. Thanks for helping. With Mom," I said, throwing the house keys to Lauren so she could open the door.

"You don't need to thank me. I care for your mother."

"I'm being polite. Shut up and let me." The second statement pretty much negated the first, but he seemed more amused than put out. Maybe he was getting used to my particular flavor of charm.

"It's quite fine. If you'd like, I'll come back and get you so you can visit your mother tonight."

"I'll call you. Wait, you don't have a cell phone, do you?" He shook his head. Of course he didn't. Stupid Luddite vampires. "God, you fangers are so out of touch. Mom's got hers in her coat pocket at the hospital. I'll call it and let you know if I need a pick-up, okay?"

"Fine." He watched me hop down to the ground. "When things are improved, I'll help you with your new gift. You might not have it forever, but while you do, you might as well grasp its nuances."

"I'm pretty sure I got this. If you didn't get the memo, I kick ALL the asses," I said.

He smiled faintly. "Oh, you do, but half of this conversation you're saying aloud, half is in my head, so I think there are a few areas in need of improvement."

That took the wind out of my sails. I grunted, tossing him a wave before following Lauren into the house. The second I stepped in, I wished I'd stayed out. It smelled like Chinese food heave in the living room. Why couldn't I cry like a normal chick? That was so much more sanitary.

"Oh, my God. So friggin' gross," I said, but Lauren shrugged and disappeared into the kitchen.

"It's nasty, but it doesn't bother me all that much. Being dead has a few benefits after all." If she wanted to spin that as a perk, I wasn't going to stop her. Zombie power, yo. Represent.

Between the two of us, we got the house into shape within the hour. As I wrapped up the trash, I found myself smiling at Lauren's back. I never would have guessed that I'd like having her around so much. She was nice, she'd helped my mom, and having someone nearby that could bench press Toyotas was bound to be handy. Pickle jars would never again be an issue.

"Thanks for what you did last night, Lauren. Lubov would have pasted me without your help."

"Oh, it was nothing. Well, it was scary, but at least I learned that not everything is awful about being dead. I can be useful."

I patted her shoulder in my best empathy overture yet. Sainthood was an 'Atta girl' away. "You don't look dead. Like, you don't have to tell people you are, you know. It's not like you smell or look rotten or whatever. You could go out and do human stuff and it won't be a thing. They might think you're sick with your skin tone, but who cares?"

"Maybe one day." She hauled the trash toward the porch, pausing in the doorway to smile at me. "Dr. Dempsey wants to monitor me to make sure that I won't go brains-crazy. When we know that, maybe I can look into doing person stuff again."

"That'd be cool."

"Yeah, it would."

Between the fight yesterday, the hospital stay, and the housecleaning, I smelled. I couldn't shower thanks to my bandages, but I could bathe, so I claimed the bathroom in the name of destinkification. My limited range of motion made it tougher than it needed to be; by the time I dressed myself an hour later, I was in a full-blown snit. Shirts and bras were impossible. So were socks. I had to settle for fuzzy pajama pants with an elastic waist and an oversized tee shirt.

Brushing my hair was equally as annoying. I couldn't lift my arms for very long, so every tangle was a slice of personal Hell. I was two second away from shaving my head when the doorbell rang. My gut promptly dropped to my knees. I'd killed the vampire leader of Boston. It wasn't so farfetched to think that one of his monster friends might come calling. I traded out the comb for a Glock, easing my way toward the front window, the gun pressed against my thigh.

A silver BMW glinted at me from the driveway. I shoved the weapon into my desk drawer and ran for the stairs, taking them two at a time. I wanted to tackle Ian when I opened the door, but he stood there with a tray of coffee and food so he was spared any monkey business.

"Hey!"

"'Sup?" He offered me a kiss, and I greedily accepted, my hands cupping his cheeks to hold him close. He chuckled and pulled away, tongue slicking over his bottom lip like he wanted to capture my taste. It made me want to kiss him again.

"You're supposed to be at school," I said, stepping aside so he could come in. "I mean, I'm super happy to see you, but this is a surprise."

"I told my 'rents what happened and asked if I could skip. They were fine with it and sent your mom their best. They're weird, but pretty nice most of the time." He put the coffee and food on the table and turned to eye my injuries, frowning when he saw the bandages crisscrossing my chest. He reached out to trace the one at my shoulder but pulled back at the last second, like he was afraid he'd hurt me.

"I won't break," I said, stepping up to hug him, my arms wrapping around his waist. He did his best not to touch anything battered, which meant his hands ended up on my butt because it was the only part of me not sporting a cut or bruise.

We stood like that awhile, his lips grazing my wet hair. It felt good—no, not good. Perfect. Whenever he was near, a part of me wanted to wriggle on the floor like an excited puppy. I wouldn't 'cause that was dumb, but I thought about it a lot. And thinking about it made me happy.

"I dunno why you keep coming back around, but I'm glad you do," I said.

"Stop saying that. I like hanging with you. You're different."

"You mean I'm weird as shit."

Ian poked me in the butt. "No, I mean, you're real and interesting. It bugs me when you say that 'cause it makes me think you believe you're broken."

I didn't know how to tell him he was wrong. I was socially awkward, I didn't have a lot of friends. My mom was a whackjob, my career trajectory lent itself to close encounters with the freak kind. I had to shoot a person last night and I didn't feel bad about it which made me think I might be Hannibal Lecter in training.

Didn't that sound broken? Maybe he didn't know me well enough to see how deep the damage went.

"You're thinking too hard," he said, as if reading my thoughts.

"Huh?"

He pressed at a spot between my eyebrows with his thumb. "You get a wrinkle here. My mom gets it. My dad says she's thinking too hard when he sees it."

Okay, so maybe he knew me a little. I smiled and he leaned down to kiss me again, but when his lips were about to touch mine, he paused, so close I could feel his breath on my face. "I know you think you're weird. But it's a good weird, okay? You're awesome." And then his mouth was on mine and my hands were on his shoulders. We kissed until I forgot how to breathe, and when he pulled back and I looked into his face, seeing the smile there, my fears faded.

Ian did know me. He knew me because he said I was awesome. And I was awesome. Maggie Cunningham, The Awesome.

Fuck yeah.

EPILOGUE

EIGHT WEEKS LATER, things were normal. Normal-ish. Janice dyed her hair teal with orange tips and, for reasons I didn't understand, had gotten a tattoo of a cupcake on her shoulder that she showed to anyone stupid enough to stand still for too long. Bankers, gas attendants, grocery clerks—it didn't matter. All hail the cupcake *or else*.

She couldn't move her neck in certain ways during recovery, so we kept to one and two star gigs for income. Ghost evictions, sprite exterminations. After killing Max, I was up for my journeyman's license, but I wouldn't take my test for a couple more weeks. I had a lot of studying to do before then. It wasn't all silver and stakes. There were laws and DoPR protocol to know, too.

Mom had never been much of a hostess, but come July, she got the brilliant idea to have a barbecue. Jeff, Lubov, Julie, John, and Ian would join me, Mom, and Lauren for "Fun, Food, and Fuckery" as Mom put on the invitations. I sweated it because this was the first time Ian would see Mom post-accident. My one consolation was that the only way their third introduction could out-suck the previous two was if somebody spontaneously combusted.

"So what time's Ian getting here?" Mom asked for the zillionth time.

I speed-chopped watermelon while Lauren arranged them into artful rows on a platter. I wanted to point out that we'd eat it, not take pictures of it, but she seemed so happy playing zombie Martha Stewart, I left her alone. Besides, we'd already had to take her off of meat duty; for every pound of hamburger patties assembled, she'd eat two pounds of raw materials. She was an expensive commodity on the barbecue assembly line.

"Never, Mom. He's never coming. And every time you ask he's going to take that much longer to never get here."

She biffed me upside the head with the paper towels. "I didn't raise you to be such a smart-ass, Margaret Jane."

"It's Maggie. Why do you insist upon calling me that? Do you hate me?"

"I don't. I love you." Janice wrapped her arms around me from behind and gave me a firm squeeze. "You're my favorite daughter. I almost never resent that it took twenty-three hours to launch you from my loins or that you gave me hemorrhoids my last trimester."

"Gee, Mom. Thanks. Stop touching me now. I have a knife." I flashed it near her eye. She laughed.

"You'd never use it on me. You love your mommy too much." She was right, but that didn't stop me from threatening matricide anyway. Other people expressed affection with warm sentiments and kisses. I used death threats and demeaning language. Don't judge.

Mom grabbed a package of hotdogs and scratched her head, looking like she forgot whatever it was she wanted to do. "What'd I... oh right."

"Huh?"

"Nothing."

She ducked around the corner to play with the stereo. A loud, hard guitar chord prefaced a high-pitched "I'm Back" scream, signaling the start of "Back in the Saddle Again." Lauren bobbed to it beside me. I waggled and waited for Janice to tell me if she wanted pasta salad or potato salad first, but she didn't return to the kitchen. I wandered into the living room only to stop dead in my tracks. Mom stood on the coffee table, ass pointed in my direction, her hips gyrating back and forth with every clap of drum. The hotdogs were a makeshift microphone as she faux-shrieked with Steven Tyler.

"Mom, don't climb on the furniture. Are you nine? Get down."

She ignored me to do a half-pirouette thing. In the minute she'd been out of my sight, she'd evolved into the Lord of the Dance.

"Janice, get off the..."

Another butt wiggle. Oh, good. And now we rocked out with air guitar.

"Mom."

She pointed the hotdogs at me like I was supposed to sing into the cased meat.

"Mooooom."

Before I could bitch at her that the last thing I needed was for Ian to see her like this, yet furthering his impression that she was some space reject, she dragged me up onto the table beside her and danced, bumping her bony hip at mine. I oomphed and glared as I nearly toppled over, and she leaned in to inform me that a snake was going to rattle?

"What the crap is wrong with you?"

Her answer, of course, was to blow me a kiss. Everything was wrong with her, and probably me by extension. But as the music played on and I danced with her on the table, I realized I was more okay with that than I thought. Because I was awesome.

THE awesome, thank you very much.

ACKNOWLEDGEMENTS

ACKNOWLEDGING EVERY PERSON who helps me write is nigh impossible. I'm surrounded by family and friends whose support makes this crazy career a reality, so here we go short and sweet:

Humans, I adore you. Friend humans and family humans and industry humans who see to it that my brain meats are able to hurl words onto a page, I couldn't do it without you. You know who you are, you know you are loved and appreciated. Thank you from the bottom of my black, shriveled heart.

That squared, I'd like to call attention to one particular human, without whom this book wouldn't be possible. Maggie Cunningham is a bold girl who perseveres despite the odds. She's not afraid to speak her mind. She's not afraid to put her foot down and say NO. She's aware she's not perfect and she's secure in her own skin in spite of it.

The influence upon her is transparent: Janice teaches Maggie to respect her voice, her body, and in turn, herself. Those lessons came directly from my mother to me. Without my mom, Maggie wouldn't be possible. Mom's fierce. She's fought for everything she has and always comes out on top. If people take anything away from this book (beyond the bawdy humor and a few new and creative curse words) it's that the world isn't ever going to validate you, so you better get good at doing it yourself. There's no shame in knowing your worth as a human being—in knowing how awesome you really are.

Thanks, Mom, from me and Maggie. We couldn't have done it without you.

The
Devil is
quitting...

THE DEVIL'S APPRENTICE

JAN SIEGEL

...but who's
taking over?

THE DEVIL'S APPRENTICE

When Pen inherits the job of caretaker for a London building with no doors and only a secret entrance from the caretaker's lodge – which she must never use – little does she know it will lead her into unbelievable danger. For Azmordis, also known as Satan, a spirit as old as Time and as powerful as the Dark, immortality is running out.

In the house with no front door, a group of teenagers are trapped in assorted dimensions of myth and history, undergoing the trials that will shape them to step into his cloven footwear – or destroy them. Assisted by an aspiring teenage chef called Gavin and Jinx, a young witch with more face-piercing than fae-power, Pen must try to stop the Devil's deadly game – before it's too late.

'Jan Siegel is probably the best British fantasy writer working today, and *The Devil's Apprentice* is, true to form, a box of delights. It is entirely unmissable.'

Lavie Tidhar, World Fantasy Award-winning author

'She writes in a quiet but uncommonly witty style that can soar into elegance or mute dread.'

Publishers Weekly on *The Witch Queen*

TOGETHER THEY FACED
THE END OF THE WORLD...

THE
GARDEN OF
DARKNESS

GILLIAN MURRAY KENDALL

Their families dead from the pandemic SitkaAZ13, known as "Pest," 15-year-old cheerleader Clare and 13-year-old chess club member Jem are thrown together. They realize that, if either of them wishes to reach adulthood, they must find a cure. A shadowy adult broadcasting on the radio to all orphaned children promises just that – to cure children once they grow into Pest, then to feed and care for them.

Or does this adult have something else in mind? Against a hostile landscape of rotting cities and a countryside infected by corpses and roamed by voracious diseased survivors, Jem and Clare make their bid for life and, with their group of fellow child-travelers growing, embark on a journey to find the cure. But they are hampered by the knowledge that everything in this new world had become suspect – adults, alliances, trust, hope. But perhaps friendship has its own kind of healing power.

THE FIRE CHILDREN

Lauren Roy